P9-DGI-981

"Debranne, I've Got A Proposition For You...."

No, dammit, not a proposition, a proposal! Kurt scowled at his reflection in the mirror, one side of his face covered with lather, as he tried to compose a brief, carefully worded proposal of marriage that could not possibly be construed as a declaration of love.

He had decided that genuine liking mixed with a hefty dose of lust was not too bad a basis for a marriage. Especially considering the fact that so many marriages based on undying love ended up on the rocks.

Right. So he would start by pointing out that fact, and then he would say, "So you see, we're not talking romance here. All I'm looking for is a simple, straightforward, mutually beneficial agreement."

The shower droned on, the mirror steamed up. Kurt swore and cleared a patch with his forearm. "Jeez," he muttered. "How could any woman in her right mind refuse a proposal like that?"

Three very different sexy bachelors say "I do!" You met the tall one in *Alex and the Angel* (September 1995), the dark one in *The Beauty, the Beast and the Baby* (March 1996); now meet the handsome one!

Dear Reader,

The holidays are always a busy time of year, and this year is no exception! Our "banquet table" is chock-full of delectable stories by some of your favorite authors.

November is a time to come home again—and come back to the miniseries you love. Dixie Browning continues her TALL, DARK AND HANDSOME series with *Stryker's Wife*, which is Dixie's 60th book! This MAN OF THE MONTH is a reluctant bachelor you won't be able to resist! Fall in love with a footloose cowboy in *Cowboy Pride*, book five of Anne McAllister's CODE OF THE WEST series. Be enthralled by *Abbie and the Cowboy*—the conclusion to the THREE WEDDINGS AND A GIFT miniseries by Cathie Linz.

And what would the season be without HOLIDAY HONEYMOONS? You won't want to miss the second book in this cross-line continuity series by reader favorites Merline Lovelace and Carole Buck. This month, it's a delightful wedding mix-up with *Wrong Bride, Right Groom* by Merline Lovelace.

And that's not all! *In Roared Flint* is a secret baby tale by RITA Award winner Jan Hudson. And Pamela Ingrahm has created an adorable opposites-attract story in *The Bride Wore Tie-Dye*.

So, grab a book and give *yourself* a treat in the middle of all the holiday rushing. You'll be glad you did.

Happy reading!

Lucia Macro

Senior Editor
and the editors of Silhouette Desire

Please address questions and book requests to:
Silhouette Reader Service
U.S.: 3010 Walden Ave., P.O. Box 1325, Buffalo, NY 14269
Canadian: P.O. Box 609, Fort Erie, Ont. L2A 5X3

DIXIE
BROWNING
STRYKER'S WIFE

SILHOUETTE *Desire*

Published by Silhouette Books
America's Publisher of Contemporary Romance

If you purchased this book without a cover you should be aware
that this book is stolen property. It was reported as "unsold and
destroyed" to the publisher, and neither the author nor the
publisher has received any payment for this "stripped book."

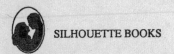

SILHOUETTE BOOKS

ISBN 0-373-76033-7

STRYKER'S WIFE

Copyright © 1996 by Dixie Browning

All rights reserved. Except for use in any review, the reproduction
or utilization of this work in whole or in part in any form by any
electronic, mechanical or other means, now known or hereafter
invented, including xerography, photocopying and recording, or in
any information storage or retrieval system, is forbidden without
the written permission of the editorial office, Silhouette Books,
300 East 42nd Street, New York, NY 10017 U.S.A.

All characters in this book have no existence outside the imagination of
the author and have no relation whatsoever to anyone bearing the same
name or names. They are not even distantly inspired by any individual
known or unknown to the author, and all incidents are pure invention.

This edition published by arrangement with Harlequin Books S.A.

® and TM are trademarks of Harlequin Books S.A., used under license.
Trademarks indicated with ® are registered in the United States Patent
and Trademark Office, the Canadian Trade Marks Office and in other
countries.

Printed in U.S.A.

Books by Dixie Browning

DIXIE BROWNING

is celebrating her sixtieth book for Silhouette since 1980 with the publication of *Stryker's Wife*. She has also written a number of historical romances with her sister under the name Bronwyn Williams. A charter member of Romance Writers of America, a member of Novelists, Inc., Browning has won numerous awards for her work. She divides her time between Winston-Salem and the Outer Banks of North Carolina.

One

Inhaling the familiar aroma of salt, diesel fuel and fish, Kurt Stryker tilted the fighting chair, propped his feet on the transom of his charter boat, the *R&R*, and sipped his first beer of the day. Life, on the whole, was good, he decided. Idly, he watched through a forest of masts and outriggers as the sun slipped slowly beneath the surface of the Atlantic.

"How many o' them things have you had?" his young mate demanded from the pier, having just arrived with their evening meal. "There's coffee in the pot if you want sump'n to drink."

"One. This is it." Kurt held up the brown bottle.

A skeptical look on his freckled face, Frog boarded the boat carrying a paper sack of burgers and fries and a king-size cola. Kurt silently cursed the drunken bastard who had spawned the kid and dragged him all over the country, leaving him with more than his share of scars. Kurt knew about scars. He had already dealt with his own, but then, his were mostly the visible kind. Frog's were the kind that had to be found before they could be healed.

"Did you pick up the mail?" he asked.

"Yeah."

"Well?"

The boy shrugged his bony shoulders. "Usual stuff."

Which meant bills. At fourteen, Frog Smith could barely read. Kurt had enrolled him in the local school, much to the boy's disgust. In their spare time, between charters and maintenance work, he tutored him in reading, math, navigation and survival skills.

Frog had already mastered a few survival skills that Kurt, after years of flying search-and-rescue missions for the U.S. Coast Guard, had never even considered. Their relationship had progressed over the past two years from combativeness through wariness to a mutual respect. And perhaps something more, at least on Kurt's part.

Frog handed over a few rumpled envelopes, and Kurt quickly scanned the return addresses. "Jones's Hardware. That'll be the paint." The *R&R* was one of the few remaining wooden charter boats along this section of the North Carolina coast. He'd bought her for a song and spent a fortune bringing her up to standard. In a year or so, he might spend another fortune on a first-class fiberglass job.

Then again, he might not. Wood was good. Classic, you might say.

He examined another envelope but didn't bother to open it. Pierce's Electronic Repair. "This one's going to bust the bank," he muttered. It took more than a compass, a flare and a few life jackets to operate legally these days.

"We broke?" There was anxiety in the boy's voice.

"Nah, we're not broke, but we're going to have to hustle if we plan to buy that house out on Oyster Point."

"Hey, who needs a house? We got us a place to live."

"*We* need a house, that's who. Anywhere else, we wouldn't get away with living aboard the *R&R*. There's rules—"

"Ah—rules is for fools," Frog said dismissively.

Shaking his head, Kurt quickly scanned the rest of the mail. No cancellations. Thank the Lord for small favors. The season was winding down. Barring storms, he still had five more charters on the book, but he was determined to make it through an entire season in the black before dipping into his retirement fund for a house that was in even worse shape than the boat had been when he'd bought it.

Actually, his first season as captain of his own boat had been pretty successful so far. He liked to think it was because he was damned good at what he did, but it probably had more to do with the fact that his rates were the cheapest along this section of the coast. The *R&R* was hardly a luxury yacht. Bottom-of-the-line carpet to cover the hatches. Ditto the plumbing fixtures. But she had a pair of dependable Detroit diesels and a hull that had been designed specifically for the waters around the Outer Banks.

"*Three* burgers? Who's the third one for?" Kurt asked as Frog ripped into the sack.

"Hey, I'm a growing kid, awright?"

"I told you you need milk with your meals, not all those colas."

"I ain't growing all *that* much." The towheaded teenager bit off a third of his first cheeseburger.

"Done your homework yet?" Kurt asked after awhile.

"Aww, man—you're worse'n Pa ever was."

Kurt doubted that. From what he'd been able to put together from the locals and a few of Frog's remarks, the boy's parents had migrated from somewhere out west doing odd jobs and knocking over the occasional convenience store. The mother had dropped out of sight several years ago. Nobody knew where she was. Frog and his old man had wound up at Swan Inlet, where that gentleman had found temporary work driving a fish truck. When he'd been sober enough. He'd been headed north with a load of gray trout when he'd tried to beat a fast freight train to a crossing. It was discovered during the cleanup of the ensuing wreckage that fish wasn't all he'd been transporting.

Frog had already gone to earth by the time the first social worker had come sniffing around. It had been generally assumed that he'd moved on, and that was the end of that. Three weeks later, when he was caught shoplifting food at a neighborhood supermarket, one of the locals had offered him a room and a job. The boy had declined. Claimed he was seventeen, used to being on his own.

He was fourteen. His voice was still in the process of changing. He'd been bunking aboard a dry-docked commercial fishing boat and doing odd jobs around the marina when Kurt had bought the boat right out from under him, so to speak, and had more or less inherited the kid. They were a team now. A pretty good one, although Frog didn't always agree with that assessment.

"Homework," Kurt reminded him now.

"Hell, man, you told me yourself you never got no degree. What's the big deal?"

"*Didn't* get a degree, not *never got no*. Don't swear, and we're talking high school diploma now. A diploma *is* a big deal. We'll talk about your degree later."

"If I'm still around," Frog muttered.

"You'll be around."

"Oh, yeah?"

"Yeah. Who else is going to keep me on course? One beer, no smokes and no fast women?" Kurt grinned. Slipping off his eye patch, he scratched his head where the tapes tied in back. "A man's gotta have someone he can count on when the chips are down."

Frog nodded sagely. "A guy to watch his back and see don't nobody break no bottle over his head."

Kurt didn't bother to correct his grammar. Rome wasn't built in a day. Right now he was more concerned with teaching the boy trust, responsibility and the advantages of a basic education. "You got it, kid." He held up a palm. Frog high-fived him just as a woman emerged from the fifty-five-footer on the other side of the finger pier and sent him a speculative look.

"Captain Stryker, isn't it? You took out that fishing party from Kinston? I heard you guys when you went out this morning. I was still in bed."

"Sorry if we disturbed your sleep, ma'am."

"Ma'am. That's cute. And Captain—you can disturb my sleep any old time." She smiled. She had a pretty smile. At least most people would call it pretty. For some reason, it made Kurt nervous.

"Shark off the port beam," Frog mumbled under his breath. He was grinning from ear to ear. One of his chief sources of amusement since they had teamed up had been watching women's reactions to Kurt and Kurt's reaction to women.

"Ever do any moonlight cruises?" the woman inquired, her voice laced with all sorts of possibilities.

Frog covered a snort of laughter with a grimy hand. Ignoring him, Kurt concentrated on not staring at the woman's sagging halter. What was inside it wasn't sagging. Not at all.

"Er, ah . . ." He cleared his throat.

"I've heard it can be awfully nice offshore on a calm night."

"Long's you wear plenny o' clothes. Them vampire skeeters'll be all over you the minute the wind drops off," Frog put in with a knowing snicker.

"Stow it," Kurt growled quietly. He had no intention of taking the woman up on whatever it was she was hinting at. Nevertheless, it was the captain's decision to make, not his mate's.

And the captain was single, dammit. He was male. He might be an aging, one-eyed gimp with a lousy track record where women were concerned, but that didn't mean he was out of the race. Not by a long shot. If he wanted a woman, he would damn well have one. And regardless of what he'd said earlier, he didn't need any smart-mouth kid to run interference for him.

She kept looking at him. Kurt was used to having women look at him. His nickname in college had been Handsome. Which had embarrassed the hell out of him, even more than the stuttering that had made his life miserable all through grade school.

Which was one of the reasons he was still somewhat socially retarded. His two best friends back in high school, Gus and Alex, had teased him about being shy. Their girlfriends had thought he was cute.

Cute! Judas priest. That was even worse than being shy!

He'd been a damn good football player in his high school and college days, though, which had probably accounted for his popularity with women. There was sure as hell nothing out of the ordinary about dark blond hair, gray eyes and his father's square jaw and blunt nose.

After he'd dropped out of college and joined the Coast Guard, the uniform had only seemed to add to the attraction. Unfortunately, it had been too late to do him much good. The woman he'd been in love with at the time had preferred Alex's money to Kurt's good looks or Gus's rough charm.

Dina. All three of them had been in love with her. She'd chosen Alex, and eventually, Kurt and Gus had gotten over her.

At least, Kurt had. Since then he'd gotten over a number of lesser attractions before getting involved seriously again. Then, ironically, it had been his lack of looks that had done him in. He'd still been pretty much of a physical wreck when Evelyn had left him leaning on his crutch at the altar.

Idly, he wondered what Dina and Evelyn would have made of a dinky little no-stoplight fishing village like Swan Inlet.

What would they have made of Frog? A homely kid who was all long, skinny limbs, big feet and tough talk.

He couldn't picture either one of them being content to live aboard a reconstituted commercial fishing boat with no Jacuzzi, no maid service—not even a CD player. The whole idea struck him as amusing and just a bit sad.

So, okay. Maybe he would go ahead and start the process of buying that house. He had a family now— or as much of a family as he was ever apt to have. After nearly twenty years of pulling up stakes every three years, moving from base to base—from Carolina to California, from Hawaii to Alaska to the U.S. Virgin Islands—he was more than ready to settle down.

"Captain Stryker? I'm pretty much at loose ends almost every evening," the woman in the loose halter said, her voice a husky invitation.

Kurt shifted uncomfortably in his chair. "Yes, ma'am. The thing is, I'm...uh, booked up pretty solid."

Frog smirked.

The woman sniffed.

Kurt pretended an intense interest in the rumpled statement from Pierce's Electronic Service.

Overhead, a gull flapped past with a finger mullet in his bill. Something hit the water not two feet abaft the port beam. It wasn't the finger mullet.

"Splotch alert," Frog quipped.

Kurt decided the boy's vocabulary had improved, even if his grammar hadn't. "Thanks, mate. We're covered, but maybe you'd better pass the word."

Kurt glanced up at the overhang from the flying bridge that covered a portion of the cockpit. They grinned at each other. Frog nodded toward the woman in the white shorts and halter, who was stroking her legs with after-sun lotion, her gaze straying frequently toward Kurt.

"Bet that stuff she's rubbin' on 'er ain't gull-proof."

When Kurt didn't reply, Frog noisily finished his drink and dumped the ice overboard. "Know why she keeps looking at you?"

"No, but I expect you're going to tell me."

"It's that eye patch. Makes you look like a pirate. Women like pirates."

"Oh, yeah? How would you know what women like?" They'd talked about women before. Mostly warnings on Kurt's part and bragging on Frog's.

The boy shrugged. "I notice stuff like that. What about tomorrow, you gonna let me go out?"

"That's a negative." They had talked about this subject, too. No weekday charters during school months. It was still a sore spot between them, because in season, Frog's tips could run anywhere from twenty-five to a hundred dollars a trip, depending on the length of the charter, the number of fish caught and the size and generosity of the party. Kurt had insisted on starting a savings account for him, much to the boy's disgust.

"How you gonna run the boat and wait on fishermen? You need me, man."

"What I need is a partner who can read a chart, lay out a course and follow it. What I need—"

"Awright, awright! So maybe I'll just shove off and try my luck somewheres else where I don't have to learn all that crap."

It wasn't the first time he'd threatened to leave. Kurt could only hope he didn't mean it. He had no hold on the boy. No legal hold. "Anyhow," Kurt said, "this Kiley fellow's not a fisherman, he's a photographer. No hooks to be baited."

"So who's gonna put film in his camera and hand over his fancy bottled water when he wants a swig?"

"Nice try, kid." Kurt chuckled. Another crisis avoided. "Now go below and get started on your homework. I'll be down directly to check you out."

It had taken two years, but Debranne Eliza Ellen Kingsly Kiley, called Deke by most of her friends, was on her way. Finally!

"Funeral, here I come," she muttered, and was mildly shocked by her own irreverence.

Her husband's first funeral had been a circus. His brother had planned it with no input at all from her. Not that she'd been up to it at the time. She'd still been in shock.

Once she'd been able to think again, she had thought about having her own private memorial on the first anniversary of the occasion, but when the time had come she'd been sick with stomach flu that had dragged on for weeks, so she'd postponed her plans for another year. A year and six weeks wouldn't do. Deke was cursed with an orderly mind, which meant that anniversaries came annually, not any old time it was convenient.

So now it was the second anniversary, and she was in perfect health. This time, she was determined to see it through. The champagne alone had cost nearly a week's rent, but it was Mark's favorite kind. While she was at it she had splurged on a pair of beautiful, brand-new crystal champagne glasses, too, because Mark had also appreciated fine crystal.

The leis had been even harder to find than the champagne, but as they had honeymooned in Hawaii, leis had seemed a fitting floral tribute.

So now she was on her way. She refused to think about those nasty whispers she had overheard a few weeks after Mark's death, about his wandering eye. He'd been too busy building an empire for any extra-curricular hanky-panky.

Goodness, he'd hardly had time for his own wife, and they'd still been in the honeymoon stage.

To clear her mind of unworthy thoughts, Deke went over her checklist. She had been taught early and well that orderliness was right up there alongside cleanliness, which was right next door to godliness. "Camera case, notebook, overnight bag—check! Champagne, glasses, leis—check!"

And then she moved on to her next list. Lights off, stove off, windows locked, door locked. Done, done, done and done.

Orphaned at the age of thirteen, Deke Kingsly Kiley could barely remember her father, who had died when she was five, but she'd never felt a lack of love. She'd been brought up by a mother who found life rather overwhelming, and by three elderly women whose notion of propriety had been formed during the Coolidge administration. She had loved them all dearly, and they had loved her right back. Although she had to admit that none of them had left her particularly well prepared for life as a single woman in the nineties. The nineteen nineties, that is.

Still, she'd made it. She was doing just fine, thank you. She had two published books to her credit, another one under contract, a part-time job at a daycare center and another one at Biddy's Birdery, feeding baby birds and cleaning cages.

Not to mention one brief marriage.

Three and a half years ago she had married a handsome, highly successful businessman from nearby Norfolk. Mark Kiley had owned the shopping mall where she'd been signing her first book. He'd seen her there and stopped by to ask how it was going, and one thing had led to another. A week later, on their third date, he told her that her serenity and her quaint, old-fashioned beauty had knocked him clean off his pins.

Two weeks later they'd been married.

Her great-aunts had been horrified. A year's engagement was *de rigeur*, Aunt Ellen had insisted. Anything less was hardly even decent, according to Aunt Eliza.

If Granna Anne hadn't passed away the previous spring, Deke might never have been allowed to marry, because Anne Kingsly had been nobody's pushover. Of all the Kingsly women—Deke's mother, Deborah, her grandmother, Anne, and her two great-aunts, Eliza and Ellen, Granna Anne had been the only one with any backbone at all. Deke liked to think she had inherited it, but there were times when she wondered, she truly did.

Hers had been a storybook romance. Unfortunately, it hadn't had a storybook ending. No happily ever after. She'd been so sure that once her family got to know Mark they would love him as much as she did, only there hadn't been time. First Great-aunt Ellen had died, and then, in less than a year, Great-aunt Eliza had died. Mark had been too busy overseeing a huge development off the coast of South Carolina to help Deke deal with her grief. Not to mention dealing with all the legal red tape of a joint will that had been written before Deke had even been born.

She had begged Mark to help her. He'd promised to look into it just as soon as he could spare a minute. He was always incredibly busy, but then, one of the things that had attracted her in the first place had been his ambition. His aggressiveness. It had been enormously appealing to a woman who'd been trained from the cradle to be pretty, polite and passive.

It had been shortly after that that she'd seen the advertisement for a mail-order course in self-empowerment and assertiveness. If she hadn't been so worried about her marriage—the gloss seemed to have gone off rather quickly—and overwhelmed by all the legal hocus-pocus she was hearing from her great-aunt's executor—not to mention her concerns about her second book, which wasn't coming along as it should...

If it hadn't been for all that, she never would have sent off for the blasted thing.

Not that it had helped much. When it worked at all it was in fits and spurts, usually when she least expected it. She still blamed Lesson Two for what happened when she'd asked Mark if they could please start a family. Empowerment is the birthright of every woman, the first paragraph had stated. It is important to express your needs in unequivocal language.

So she had. An only child, Deke had desperately wanted babies of her own. She'd said so.

Mark had laughed. He'd told her she was child enough for him, and that it was about time she grew up because she was beginning to bore him with her childish demands.

That had hurt her feelings. With all the dignity and empowerment she could summon, she had asked why he had married her if he hadn't wanted a family.

"Why? God knows. Maybe because you were a virgin and that's a pretty rare commodity in this day and age."

"You couldn't possibly have known that—not then, at least."

"Ah, come on, honey, you were practically advertising the fact. The way you dressed—the way you talked—even the way you sat there, with your knees together and your feet flat on the floor, like you were scared to death a fly would buzz up your petticoat."

It wasn't true. None of it. Oh, it was true enough that she'd been a virgin, but she'd been wearing a sophisticated new outfit, a new hairstyle and a new shade of lipstick in honor of her very first autographing when they'd met.

Besides, things like that didn't show...did they? "I don't believe you," she'd said flatly.

Mark had sneered. There was no other way to describe it. "You were a novelty, darling, but let's face it—novelties wear off, so be a good little girl and get off my back, will you?"

That was when the mail-order course had kicked in. She'd thrown a vase of roses at him. A Steuben vase.

It had been a wedding gift, and Mark had known to the penny how much it had cost, which she'd thought rather crass at the time, but of course, by then, her training had quit cold on her, so she hadn't told him so.

Never go to bed angry. That, along with that business about turning the other cheek, was one of her great-aunts' favorite sayings.

So Mark had slammed out, and Deke had waited up, unable to sleep until she had apologized and smoothed things over between them.

He hadn't come home at all. The next day his partner had called to tell her that Mark had gone out of town on another business trip and wouldn't be home until the following Tuesday.

Still furious, hurt and determined to get over both, she had applied herself to packing away her great-aunts' clothing to give to the church's Helping Hand Society.

And then word came that Mark had been killed in a plane crash.

Deke had run the gamut of emotions. Remorse, regret, anger, denial, grief—although not necessarily in that order. Suddenly, she'd found herself completely alone, without family and dangerously short on resources. In the midst of all that, poor old Mr. Hardcastle, her own family lawyer, had come to inform her that he had finally finished settling her great-aunts' convoluted estate, and that, my how he wished he had insisted they update their will, but then, the Misses Ellen and Eliza had been a law unto themselves, hadn't they?

The Kingsly home place, where Deke and her father and his entire family had grown up, was now the property of a distant cousin from Cleveland, who intended to put it on the market immediately because he needed the money.

The furniture was to be auctioned off, all except for one or two personal bequests.

On the heels of dealing with all that had come the news that the house she had shared with Mark had been leased in the name of the jointly owned development firm, of which Mark's older brother, Hammond, was not only the legal counsel, but senior partner and major shareholder.

Deke had blamed herself for not becoming more informed while there'd still been time. She had blamed that darn course in self-assertiveness for letting her down and for her last quarrel with Mark. She still felt guilty over that. It was the last time she had ever seen him.

However, having no other choice, she had picked up the pieces and got on with her life. Not particularly gracefully, but at least she'd managed to deal with things as they came.

And boy, had they come! The minute word of Mark's death got out, people she had never even met had swarmed all over her, taking over, talking over her head, going though things, shoving papers under her nose for her to sign. Hammond, who might have been more supportive, had been among the worst.

After all three estates had been finally settled with all the whereases and heretofores and bequeathings—goodness, the process took forever!—Deke had ended up with her husband's camera and his last name, and her grandmother's parlor organ, which was seven feet tall and weighed a ton.

Not that she could play a note, because she couldn't. And even if she could, the bellows wheezed, but all the same, she appreciated the sentiment.

By then, of course, she had been informed that although state law allowed the widow a portion of her late husband's assets, when those assets were corporate assets, and the corporation was privately held by a partner who was not only a lawyer but a relative, and when her late husband had allowed his life insurance to lapse rather than pay the premiums that had increased dramatically when it was discovered that both his blood pressure and his cholesterol levels were in the stratosphere—why, then, there was really nothing much the state could do.

Deke hadn't pushed. She'd still been feeling guilty on too many counts, including the fact that once the initial shock had worn off, she'd been more angry than grieved.

It had been the most hectic period in her life, what with everything piling on at once. Tomorrow would be the second anniversary of the day Mark's plane had gone down off a place called Swan Inlet, killing him and the secretary who'd been traveling with him. The time had come to bid a proper farewell to her late husband and get on with the rest of her life.

Unfortunately, it was easier said than done.

She scanned the two-lane highway ahead for a gas station. Her car was a guzzler, which was probably why it had been so cheap. She blamed her great-aunts for not teaching her such practical things as how to deal with bankers and lawyers and nosy reporters. She blamed Mark for not teaching her practical things like how to shop for a reliable secondhand car. And she blamed herself for trying to blame others for her own shortcomings.

Maybe she should shop for a mail-order course for handling guilt.

It was late in the afternoon by the time she checked into Swan Inlet's one and only motel. Fortunately, it wasn't one of the costlier chains. This entire project was beginning to erode her meager savings rather badly.

Before setting out to locate Captain Stryker and his boat, to make sure that everything was on schedule, she washed her face and brushed her straight, shoulder-length hair, tying it back with a narrow black ribbon. Not for the first time she wished she'd been born with black hair. Or red, or platinum blond. Anything but plain old brown. The next time she broke out in a rash of self-assertiveness, she just might march down to Suzzi's Beauty Boutique and get it cut, bleached and frizzed to a fare-thee-well before she came to her senses.

Kurt was on the flying bridge hanging out laundry because the marina's dryer was on the blink again when a woman pulled up in a spray of gravel. He noticed her right off because her car obviously needed a ring job. And then he noticed her because of the way she was dressed. Most women around these parts dressed pretty casually. It was that kind of place.

This one was wearing a dress. Not just any dress, but a floaty, flower-printed thing with a lace collar. The kind of dress he could picture his mother wearing to teach Sunday school back when he was a kid.

She had a plain face. Not homely, just plain.

Although she couldn't be much more than five feet tall, there was nothing at all plain about her body.

She picked her way carefully out along the finger pier, dodging the clutter of lines, buckets and shoes. And the cracks. She was wearing high heels.

"Excuse me, sir, but do you know where I can find a Captain Stryker?"

"You found him." Kurt dropped the pair of briefs he'd been about to pin to the line and waited. She smiled then, and he decided maybe she wasn't so plain, after all.

"Oh. Well, I'm Deke Kiley. Debranne Kiley? I wrote you—I sent a check? For tomorrow?"

From the hatch just behind him, Frog said softly, "I thought you said you was taking out some camera guy tomorrow."

Deke Kiley. D.E.E. Kiley. That had been the name on the check. The stationery had been plain. No letterhead. If she was a Deke, then he was a blooming hibiscus. "Yeah, I got it. You're on." And under his breath, he said, "Pipe down, pea brain. She's a paying customer."

"Yes, well...I'll see you tomorrow morning then," the woman called out in a soft little voice that reminded him of something from the distant past. "I just wanted to be sure which boat was yours," she went on. "Eight o'clock, is that all right?"

Kurt nodded. It wasn't all right, but it would have to do. A charter was a charter, and if some lace-trimmed lady photographer wanted to snap pictures of dolphins, he reckoned her money was as green as anyone else's.

"Hey!" he yelled after her. She stopped and swiveled around and he remembered what it was she reminded him of. The ballerina on a tinkling little music box that used to sit on his mama's dressing table. "Wear sneakers tomorrow, okay?"

She smiled and nodded, and Kurt watched her swish her shapely little behind down the wharf, climb into a yellow clunker about the size of an aircraft carrier and drive off.

Semper paratus, man. The Coast Guard's motto was *Always Prepared.* Kurt had a feeling he just might not be prepared for this one.

Two

The widow wore black. Black slacks and a black silk blouse, bought especially for the occasion. She also wore a faded yellow sweatshirt because it had turned cooler than expected. Her shoes were red high tops, which weren't exactly proper funeral attire, but she wore them anyway because Captain Stryker had said to. And Deke, while she was no great sailor—had never been on a boat in her life, in fact—was savvy enough to know that a boat was no place for high heels.

She was heading out to the pier carrying the basket, her purse and her camera bag when a lanky, freckle-faced boy emerged from Captain Stryker's boat and hurried to meet her.

"Gimme that," he said, and she wondered fleetingly if he was robbing her. "Watch yer step—there's ropes and stuff."

Deke let him take the basket. He would hardly be warning her of hazards if he was planning on mugging her. Any mugger worth his salt would have grabbed her purse and camera case first. The camera alone was worth a couple of thousand dollars. It had belonged to Mark. It was one of the two things he had left her, which was just fine, because she hadn't married him for his money.

Three things, if you counted a nagging sense of disappointment.

The boy handed her down into the boat with an old-world courtliness that Deke found oddly touching.

"Thank you," she murmured.

He flashed her a grin and leapt onto the pier. "Gotta run," he said just as someone spoke from behind her.

"Miss that school bus, boy, and you're road kill."

"Aye, sir!"

Turning, Deke encountered the man she had seen only from a distance the day before. Tall, tanned, lean and blond, he would have been the handsomest man in captivity without the eye patch. With it, he was quite simply devastating. And not entirely because, as a writer of children's adventure stories, she was partial to pirates.

"Captain Stryker?"

Kurt nodded. "Ms. Kiley."

"I'm early."

"A few minutes."

The words meant nothing. Kurt sized up his passenger. She was tiny. Looked as if a stiff breeze could capsize her. Good thing he didn't charge by the pound.

Still, a charter was a charter. Every one added a few more bucks to the house fund. In case the child welfare people wanted to make a federal case about his casual arrangement with the boy, he needed to get them off the *R&R* and settled in a real house as soon as possible. That ought to weigh in his favor.

"I'll set your gear below," he offered, reaching for the basket, from which the neck of a dark green bottle protruded. "You didn't have to bring your own rations. Sandwiches and drinks are included in the price of the charter."

She murmured something he didn't quite catch, mainly because he was too busy checking her out. Yesterday he'd thought she was plain. Just went to show you the dangers of making snap judgments. She was plain the way a sunrise over a frozen bay was plain.

He settled her in one of the three fighting chairs bolted to the deck and headed topside. Frog had cast off before he'd jogged out to meet the school bus. "You need any sunscreen?" he called down over the muffled throb of the wet exhaust.

She twisted around and glanced up at the flying bridge. She had a nice smile. Simple, uncomplicated. She was probably a nice woman, he thought as he eased out into the harbor. Attractive, nice . . . and already spoken for, if the plain gold band on her third finger, left hand, was anything to go by.

Not that he was interested.

They were well beyond the breakwater, headed for open sea, when he sensed her presence on the ladder behind him. Some passengers weren't content to stay put and let him get on with his job. That was where Frog came in. For a streetwise kid who was, in the parlance, "known to the authorities" in several states, he was surprisingly good with people.

Kurt wasn't. He hoped she hadn't followed him topside looking for conversation.

She was hanging on to the ladder, her eyes wide, her face a little too pale. "Do you know the place where that plane went down a couple of years ago?" She had to raise her voice over the sound of the engines.

"Wreck Rock? Yeah, I know it," he called over his shoulder.

"Is it very far?"

"About a thirty-minute run on a good day."

"Is this a good day?"

Kurt was tempted to say it was looking better all the time, which surprised him, because he wasn't into that sort of thing. "Yeah, this is a pretty good day if you don't count the tropical depression that spun off the west coast of Africa a few days ago."

"Africa?" She looked puzzled, faintly worried.

"Forget it. This late in the season, it'll probably fizzle before it even hits the Leewards."

She still looked puzzled, making him wish he'd kept his answer brief and to the point. "Oh. Well, could we go there? The plane crash site, I mean—not Africa."

Ditzy.

Nice. Attractive in a quiet way, but definitely ditzy.

"Sure, but tell me first, are we talking dolphin, as in the fish? Dorado? Mahimahi? Or dolphin, as in the mammal? What we call porpoise. The bottle-nose. Because if it's the fish you want, I can take you to a place where you're more apt to find 'em. Wreck

Rock's too new. Takes time to build up a good feeding reef.''

"Oh, but—''

She was a distraction, but he couldn't very well ignore her. Besides, she looked as if she could do with some distraction herself. She was beginning to turn a bit green about the gills.

The roll up on the bridge was more pronounced. He wanted to suggest that she go below and watch the wake, but she looked so...needy. It was the first word that popped into his mind. So he tried his hand at distraction. "Now, if it's fish you're interested in, there might be a few sheepshead around the place where that jerk from Virginia and his mistress went down. Not as much sport as billfish or big blues, but good eating. Real good eating. We might even run into a few tuna, too, speaking of good eating.''

Maybe speaking of eating wasn't such a hot idea. She was looking sicker by the minute.

"I beg your pardon,'' she said, just as if she weren't fighting to hang on to her breakfast, "but the plane that went down happened to belong to a well-known businessman. The person traveling with him was his secretary, not his—''

He saw her swallow hard, saw a film of sweat break out on her upper lip. He was sympathetic, but never having been seasick, he couldn't exactly share her misery. "If you say so. I didn't know 'em personally, you understand—it happened before I moved to Swan Inlet, but folks around here knew 'em both. They used to fly in and hitch a ride out to their private love nest, according to—''

"She was his secretary," the woman called Deke said firmly, then spoiled the effect by gulping and moaning softly.

Oh, man. He should've offered her a patch or a pill when she'd first come aboard. Most fishermen, if they needed an anti-motion potion, brought their own, but this lady didn't look as if she'd ever set foot on a boat before.

"You want to go below and lie down?"

She took a deep breath, climbed up a couple more rungs, and to his own disgust, Kurt couldn't help noticing that as small as she was, there were some modest but intriguing curves under that sweatshirt. "No, I'll be just fine. Tell me about—oh, anything. Just talk to me, take my mind off my stomach and I'll be all right." She smiled, but it was a weak effort.

"Frog—he's my mate—the kid who helped you aboard? He's also my social director. I'm not much of one for talking." He made a minor adjustment in their course and then set the squelch on his ship-to-shore radio.

"Why did you call it Wreck Rock? I didn't think there were any rocks along this part of the coast."

Kurt shrugged. "There's not, as far as I know. Just a name. Easier than calling it by the coordinates."

For several minutes she engaged in deep breathing exercises. Kurt hoped it worked. It was too late for Dramamine, and verbal distraction—at least his brand—didn't seem to be helping much. The wind was picking up, pushing an incoming tide. He quartered the seas as best he could without getting too far off course.

"I'm hoping to see the mammal, not the fish. I want to take a few pictures if we see any. And she was his secretary," the woman said belligerently. "It said so in all the reports."

That was fine with him. If she wanted to believe Noah had gone down with all hands and hooves aboard, it was no skin off his back. "Okay, Flipper the mammal it is, and she was his secretary. They spent all those weekends out at his private island, just the two of them, working on quarterly taxes." He scanned the sky, adjusted the throttle and made another minor course correction.

When she didn't argue, he cut her a sidelong glance and immediately wished he'd kept his mouth shut. He'd never been good at small talk, especially when his mind was on something else. And anyway, trying to talk a person out of being seasick was about as effective as trying to talk the tide into not rising.

What was going to come up was going to come up.

For a good-looking woman, she didn't look so good. "You want to go below and lie down?" he offered again.

"Maybe I'd better. Just for a few minutes."

Kurt set the controls and followed her below, hoping she could hold it down long enough to make it to the head. "Through the sliding door—watch the steps. Hang on and I'll get you some fresh air." That done, he deftly flipped down one of the convertible benches that served a dual purpose in the compact salon. "Head's portside, forward. Uh, that is, it's on the left, right over there. It's kind of small, but you'll find anything you need." He handed her a plastic bucket, just in case.

She lowered herself carefully, one arm clutching the pale blue bucket. There was a bruised look about her that made him want to comfort her, only he didn't know how. Wasn't sure she'd appreciate it, even if he did. The collar of her black silk shirt was rucked up in back, so he smoothed it down and patted her shoulder once, but that didn't seem like much comfort, not if she was feeling as lousy as she looked.

Kurt wondered whether to head back to port or keep going. His passenger didn't look up to making the call, so he backed out of the salon and left her there. If it was Wreck Rock she wanted, it was Wreck Rock she would get. The customer was always right.

"Lie on your left side," he called down from the open companionway. "They say it helps."

He'd heard it somewhere but didn't know if it was true or not. He did know that in a case like this, people needed to believe there was someone in charge who knew precisely what they were doing.

Dutifully, Deke turned onto her left side, which gave her a view of a shirt and a baseball cap hanging on a hook on the wall—or whatever the nautical equivalent was. It was swaying. And swaying, and swaying, and swaying.

Oh, mercy.

"'All the rivers run into the sea, yet the sea is not full,'" she whispered. "Ecclesiastes one-seven. One-six, one-five, one-four, one-three—" As a child, she'd been prone to stomach upsets. Granna Anne used to make her quote Bible verses to keep her mind off her stomach. It hadn't worked very well. Counting backward didn't work, either. She tried talking to herself. "It's almost over, Debranne. In a little while you'll have paid your proper respects to the past and be on your way home."

Wherever home was. The Victorian house where she'd grown up was gone, the furniture being pawed over by a swarm of antique dealers. The run-down apartment building where she lived now was about to be demolished to make way for new low-cost housing, which she probably wouldn't be able to afford, as she earned a few too many dollars to qualify. Her fall royalties this year had amounted to a hefty $23.11, but she had two part-time jobs, each of which paid the minimum wage, less deductions.

"Talk, don't think, you nut! Did you bring your light meter?" Talking was supposed to prevent her from thinking about that awful feeling in her belly. "I hope you brought your meter," she muttered, "because shooting on water is tricky, and you're going to have to come up with a few decent pictures if you're planning to write this whole wacko expedition off on your taxes."

Because she was going to do it. Guilt or no guilt, she fully intended to write Mark's memorial service off on her taxes. The whole blooming thing, charter, motel, mileage and all. Caught in the throes of guilt and nausea, she clutched the bucket and moaned.

But then, Mark would have approved, she reminded herself. Hadn't he written off their entire honeymoon trip because he had spent a few minutes looking over a shopping complex on Maui?

Still, she did feel guilty. Partly about the tax thing, but mostly about the fact that she hadn't really grieved as much as she should. Not that she knew what she could do about that. Evidently she was one of those people whose feelings didn't run very deep.

As for this empowerment business, she was beginning to think it was a mixed blessing. So far, all she felt was confused.

"Hey, you all right down there?" the captain called from the open companionway. He had a nice voice. A little like rusty velvet.

Goodness, that didn't even make sense! Deke managed a wobbly smile. "Fine. I'll be upstairs in a minute."

He grinned and saluted her, and she thought, *What a nice man.* Any other time she might have thought, *What a strikingly masculine, stunningly handsome man,* but right now, nice was all she craved.

Mark hadn't been nice. There, she'd admitted it. He'd been suave and sexy and Hollywood handsome, but nice?

No. Not really. At least, not after they'd been married for a few months. She'd put it down to his being so busy, so ambitious to get ahead. There'd been all those late nights at the office. All those business trips. Nearly every weekend.

With his secretary.

With his young, drop-dead-gorgeous secretary who was supposed to be such a whiz on her laptop he couldn't travel without her.

Or maybe she'd been such a whiz on *his* laptop.

Deke remembered the night Mark had taken her out to dinner for her birthday. When he'd opened his wallet for his credit card, she'd seen a little silver packet. She'd wondered at the time why he still carried a condom, but she'd been too embarrassed to ask.

All the same, she had wondered. She wondered all over again. Wondered about that and a lot of other things she had tried for too long to ignore because it wasn't seemly to think ill of the dead.

Suddenly, like watching tea leaves settle into a pattern in the bottom of a cup, a picture of her relationship with Mark came into focus. "Well...*damn!*" she whispered plaintively.

Still struggling to deal with guilt and nausea, she was overcome with anger. It never even occurred to her that the motion of the boat had changed—less forward, more up and down, with a jiggly little corkscrew action thrown in for good measure—until she heard the sound of uneven footsteps on the little ladder doohickey that led into the living room.

She sat up, still clutching the bucket. Tears streaked her cheeks, but they were tears of anger. "Are we there?" she demanded as Captain Stryker hovered over her, looking almost as stricken as she felt.

"Kiley," he said. "His name was Kiley, wasn't it?"

Numbly, Deke nodded. It was one thing to be made a fool of. It was quite another to have it become common knowledge.

It occurred to her that he looked oddly vulnerable for such a powerful man. "You should've told me to shut up and mind my own business," he growled.

She swallowed hard. Sitting up made her feel marginally more empowered, but it didn't do a thing for her seasickness. "I was taught never to tell anyone to shut up. In my family, we say hush. It, um—it sounds softer."

"But it means the same thing." He raked his fingers through his shaggy blond hair, then hooked both thumbs under his belt. "You should've said something. I'm sorry, Ms. Kiley—just as sorry as I can be."

"Hush. It's not your fault."

He grinned, looking more than ever like the hero of a pirate story in his faded, body-loving khakis. "Hush, huh? How does your family go about telling somebody to butt out and mind their own business?"

A fresh wave of nausea swept over her, but gamely she replied, "Mostly they just change the subject. Are we there yet?"

"Speaking of changing the subject? Sorry, we're only about halfway. I thought I'd better check on you. Do you need anything? Sure you don't want to head back in?"

Deke thought about how much this project was costing her. She could hardly ask for her money back just because on the way to memorializing her late husband she happened to have discovered that he was a philandering, four-flushing, lying, greedy snake in the grass.

At least he had been all of those things while he was still alive. Poor Mark. No one, she supposed, deliberately chose to be a stinker. As long as she'd come this far, she might as well pay tribute to whatever good there was in him. It would make a nice, tidy end to that particular segment of her life, and she needed that to satisfy her sense of orderliness.

"I want to go on to Wreck Rock," she said as firmly as she could, considering she was about to disgrace herself into a plastic bucket that smelled of disinfectant.

For a minute he just stood there, swaying with the motion of the boat. A shaft of sunlight slanted down through an open hatch, highlighting the golden hair on his tanned, muscular forearm.

"We'd better hustle you topside," he said, after studying her with a single sympathetic gray eye. "You're no sailor, that's pretty clear. Maybe if you suck on a cola and let the wind blow in your face, you'll feel better."

Under a thin layer of cheap indoor-outdoor carpet that served primarily to cover the twin hatches, the deck vibrated to the beat of the engines below. Kurt noticed that the atmosphere was none too fragrant. Frog had a bad habit of hanging his fishy clothes in his locker instead of tossing them out to be washed.

Bracing his bum leg against the bulkhead, he bent and slipped his arms under her slight form. She didn't protest. Probably felt too lousy to argue. Funny thing, though—Kurt had a feeling that small or not, she was nobody's pushover. He'd caught a glint in her eye, a certain tilt of her delicate chin before she'd been done in by a weak belly.

In the cockpit, with a cool northwest breeze in her face, he figured she'd come around pretty fast. "Breathe deeply," he said. "That's it, nice and steady—inhale, exhale . . . no, don't hyperventilate, just take regular breaths. You're doing fine."

Breathing lessons. Man, he'd really lost it. But damn, she smelled good. Crazy thing, considering where they were, but she reminded him of the way a cornfield smelled when the tassels were drying under a hot summer sun.

Carefully, he lowered her onto a chair, watched for a few seconds to see that she didn't keel over, then shoved an ice cold can in her hand. "Sip," he said. "Don't gulp it down. Let me get us underway again and I'll see what I can do about smoothing out the ride."

She sipped. Kurt skimmed up the ladder and took the controls again. From time to time he glanced over his shoulder. She was hanging in there, angling her face to the wind, which was beginning to kick up a few knots. They were going to be doing some pitching and yawing before they reached their destination. He hoped to hell she was up to it.

Kiley, he thought. The joker's name was Kiley, and he'd gone down with another woman. His mistress, according to the local scuttlebutt. Nobody had mentioned a wife in the background, or if they had, he hadn't paid any attention. He'd never had much of an ear for gossip.

The jerk had been married, all right. Married to a real nice lady named Deke. Which brought up two questions in Kurt's mind. Number one—what was his widow doing here?

And number two—why the hell had he needed a mistress?

Three

"**R**ight about there," he said. Resting his head against hers, Kurt pointed off to the southeast. "Nothing much to see, but according to the coordinates, this is the place where your husband and his secretary went down." He kicked himself mentally for bringing it up again. He didn't want to know about her problems. He had enough of his own. Deke Kiley was just another charter. In a few more hours she'd be history, and he'd be one bank deposit closer to having a real home for Frog, in case some busybody from social services took a notion that a working charter boat wasn't a proper home for a growing boy.

She took a deep breath, and he noticed that her color had improved. The collar of her shirt was rucked up again, but he resisted the temptation to tuck it in. Barely. She still smelled like corn tassels, soap and shampoo. He figured a guy had to be pretty deprived to be turned on by something so wholesome. Too much celibacy could be hazardous to a guy's health. Mental and otherwise.

"Right about where that gull just tipped his wings," he said, inhaling deeply.

She still looked a little shaky. Maybe on the way back in, he'd invite her up to the flying bridge. The rolling was more noticeable there, but the view was first-class. In case he failed to raise a few porpoise, maybe she'd settle for a seagoing sunset.

"Would you please hand me my basket?" she asked, and he was reminded all over again of his mother's ballerina music box. Ms. Kiley had a dainty way of speaking. Probably grew up saying yes ma'am and no ma'am to her elders.

He set the basket on the chair beside her and would have headed to the controls but she reached out and snagged his hand. "Would you mind opening my champagne? I'm not real good with these things. The bottle always overflows when I try it."

"Are you sure you want to open it? Champagne's not noted for settling stomachs."

"Oh, my belly woes are much better now."

Her belly woes. Kurt grinned and lifted the bottle from the wicker basket, then whistled soundlessly. He was no expert on vintages, but unless he was very much mistaken, this was a pretty high-priced bottle of French fizz.

He started to pop the cork with his thumbs, then thought better of it. She could hardly finish it off alone, and it would be a shame to let it go flat. Carefully, he eased the cork out and handed it to her. She could sniff it or stick it in her pocket, it didn't matter to him.

"You pour," she said, holding up two tulip glasses that glinted like wet ice in the hazy sunlight.

"I'm driving, but thanks, anyway."

"I want to drink a toast. I can't do it alone."

Shrugging, Kurt poured both glasses a third full and handed her one. The little lady was a bundle of surprises. He had a feeling she wouldn't like being referred to as a little lady, but that was the term that came to mind when he looked at her. Little, and a lady. In the best sense of the word.

"Here's to you," he said, raising his glass.

"No, here's to all the smooth-talking, conniving, philandering cads who ever wrote off a honeymoon on their taxes." She tossed back hers and held out her glass for a refill.

Kurt lifted his eyebrows. "If you say so." He sipped. The stuff was dry as an Arizona attic. The last time he'd tasted anything like it had been at Alex and Dina's wedding reception.

"More, please." She held out her glass again. Cautiously, he splashed in a scant half inch.

Screwing her small face into a fearsome scowl, she said, "And here's to all the, um, smooth-talking—did I already say that? Well, here's to all the Lotharios who ever swept a woman off her feet and then dropped her flat on her—on her derriere with no warning."

Kurt hesitated. "Are we, by any chance, toasting your late husband?"

Deke hiccupped. "Excuse me. Don't ask personal questions."

"Lady, I didn't bring him up, you did." Dammit, he'd meant to steer clear of that particular reef.

She shrugged and looked away, and Kurt studied the delicate line of her profile. Dina, the first woman he had loved and lost, had been a tall, elegant, classically beautiful blonde. Evelyn, the woman who had left him at the altar nearly three years ago, was a tall, sexy, voluptuously gorgeous brunette.

Deke Kiley was none of the above.

Not that it mattered. Deke Kiley was a stranger, he reminded himself. She was going to remain a stranger.

Leaning over, she reached into the basket, brought out a pair of leis and proceeded to destroy them, flower by flower, tossing the torn petals overboard. Kurt watched silently for a moment and then, shaking his head, he left her and returned to the controls. She didn't even notice his leaving. The lady, he decided, was slightly screwy, but probably harmless.

Deke noticed, all right. Under the circumstances, it was unseemly, but she couldn't help noticing the way his muscles flexed as he jogged up the ladder, the way the wind blew his khakis against his muscular body.

What's more, she decided woozily, he was nice. Unusually kind, not to mention unusually attractive, even with the eye patch.

Especially with the eye patch.

What he was was sexy. Deke was no expert on sexiness in a man. She'd been taught to look for other qualities, but once a woman's hormones got in on the act, a whole new world opened up.

There'd been a time when she'd thought Mark was sexy. He had certainly managed to convince her she couldn't live without him, and vice versa. But if a woman could be married to a man for nearly eighteen months without even knowing who he was, she was nowhere near ready to trust her judgment of a man she had known for less than a day.

Besides, the last thing she needed right now was to be distracted by a sexy male rear end and a pair of tanned, golden-haired, muscular forearms. Not when she was trying so hard to be furious. Or if not furious, then certainly righteously indignant. The trouble was, her righteous indignation kept slipping away, leaving behind little more than the sour dregs of resentment and disillusionment, which hardly warranted such a dramatic, not to mention expensive, memorial.

She belched and patted her lips with a tissue. Either she was getting sick again or the mixture of champagne and cola on an empty stomach was beginning to have an effect.

Several minutes later Captain Stryker descended the ladder again. The course held steady, the prow cutting through the waves at a low rate of speed. It occurred to Deke that there was no one driving, but before she could begin to worry, she was distracted by the way he moved about the cockpit. Her slightly glazed eyes followed him with a wistful expression that would have shocked her if she'd been aware of it. She thought he must not have been in the business of chartering very long, because he hadn't quite got his sea legs yet.

Once more she admired the way his khakis hugged his rear end when he bent over to retrieve a couple more cans of cola from a locker under the ladder, and then she chided herself for noticing. Normally it was a man's hands and eyes she noticed, not his behind.

Mark's eyes had been blue, watchful and rather small.

The captain's eye was gray, deep-set and surprisingly gentle in such a harshly angular face.

Mark's hands had been elegant. He was the first man she'd ever met who had his nails professionally manicured. She'd been impressed, having been taught all her life the value of good grooming.

Captain Stryker's hands were square and tanned, with a glint of golden hairs on the back. His nails were square and short and scrupulously clean, but she'd bet her last tea biscuit that he'd never been anywhere near a manicurist.

At least not in a professional capacity.

"Hey, you want something to eat? Sandwiches? Cheese crackers?"

"Yuck." It occurred to her that she hadn't eaten since supper the night before, and very little even then. "I mean, no, thank you."

He smiled. He had nice teeth, too. Square, white but not quite perfect. She felt a vague stirring of excitement and put it down to the mixture of canned cola and French champagne and not enough food. It had to be that, because she was far too sensible to be distracted, much less attracted, by another man right now, no matter how nice his smile and his...

Well—that, too.

She had a book to finish and some major decisions to make concerning her future. In two brief years, her entire outlook on life had changed, and now she was ready to move forward. This time without any blow-dried jerk who wore silk underwear, Italian suits and too much cologne. A jerk who'd once made her feel like an idiot simply because she'd referred to his wristwatch as a Rolodex.

He'd told his brother about it, and then he'd told his secretary and a couple of developers they'd been entertaining at the club, and laughed himself silly each time.

The insensitive, self-centered bastard.

Yes! That's exactly what he'd been! The husband she'd felt so guilty over not mourning properly had been a self-centered, two-timing bastard.

Deke felt a swift surge of exhilaration in thinking a word she had never spoken aloud more than once or twice in her entire life. Profanity, she decided, helping herself to another sip of champagne, could be downright empowering.

"Bastard, bastard, bastard," she muttered. And then, while she was at it, "Damn and hell." When it came to satisfaction, assertiveness beat the heck—the hell—out of polite, ladylike passivity.

"Did you say something?" Kurt called over his shoulder.

"Nope. Nothing important."

He appeared beside her, holding out a frosty can of cola in a Souvenir of Swan Inlet sweat jacket. Removing the crystal tulip from her hand, he said, "Here, try this. It's better for what ails you than champagne."

"Nothing ails me." She flashed him a five-hundred-watt smile.

Kurt blinked. "Glad to hear it. For a minute there, I thought you might be upset about something."

Her eyes were light brown and clear as a sunlit creek. He must have just imagined that fleeting stricken look, because her grin was gutsy as all get-out. The little lady might look like a dressing-table ballerina, but underneath that dainty exterior she was pure stainless steel.

He invited her topside for a better view. "Might see a few porpoise roll by. At any rate, we're in for a pretty spectacular sunset, unless I miss my guess."

She insisted on bringing the champagne and glasses. Kurt shook his head, but when he saw that stubborn little chin of hers ratchet up another notch, he let it pass. For some people, boats and booze went together. It wasn't a mixture he cared for, having hauled too many such victims out of the drink in his air-sea rescue days, but he suspected the lady had had something of a shock today. If the champagne made it go down any easier, then who was he to complain?

He let her go up first and braced a hand on each side, in case she lost her footing. The seas weren't all that high, but they were rolling in at a pretty steady clip. He thought briefly of the latest tropical depression and then turned his attention to the view directly ahead at eye level.

Despite the cool offshore breeze, a bead of sweat trickled down his throat. By now he'd seen her from just about every angle. Looking up at her from the cockpit while she stood on the pier above him in her lace-collared, flowered dress. Looking down at her in the cabin while she lay on his bunk clutching a bucket. Looking head-on at her while they toasted whatever the hell it was they had toasted. And now this. A small, neatly rounded stern that was close enough to touch. Close enough to—

Okay, so she looked good. A little too good. Smelled good, too. Kurt was surprised and not a little alarmed at the degree of interest he was beginning to feel in a woman who wouldn't be his type, even if he'd had a type.

They were barely cruising. He'd set the controls a tad above idle. Just as she stepped onto the bridge, a rogue sea caught them on the starboard beam, and he leapt up the last few rungs. "Hang on," he warned, grabbing her with one hand and the controls with the other. She braced her small red sneakers on the textured surface, clutched the bottle and glass stem with one hand and hooked the fingers of her other hand into his belt.

It was like having a live hand grenade rammed into his pocket. He sucked in his breath and tried to ignore the sudden jolt of testosterone that shot through his system.

For the next half hour or so, Kurt regaled his passenger with everything he knew about fish, gulls and seagoing mammals. She toasted each species with a sip of champagne. He declined.

Watching carefully to see that she didn't guzzle the stuff too fast and get sick again, he searched for another topic to take her mind off whatever ailed her. He mentioned the years he'd spent doing search and rescue missions for the Coast Guard, making it sound as routine as any other job, not because he was overly modest but because he'd never been given to dramatics.

Evidently, his social skills were improving, because she sipped. She didn't guzzle. Between sips she told him about the story line she had conceived that she was hoping to sell as a proposal for her third book, then had to explain what a proposal was.

They talked about cold winters and hot summers and dogs they had once owned. He told her a little about growing up on a central North Carolina farm that was now a strip mall, and she told him about growing up in a small town near Norfolk, Virginia, with three elderly teetotaling relatives, and about the small girls' school she had attended that had taught her Latin and eighteenth-century literature but not a whole lot about surviving the twentieth century.

He caught her looking at his eye patch a few times. Evidently either her school or her elderly relatives had taught her not to ask personal questions of strangers.

So, feeling as expansive as if he'd matched her drink for drink, he told her about the crash he'd survived in rescuing a kid and a dog during a near blizzard, again not making himself out to be a hero, because he wasn't. He'd simply been a part of a team doing a job that was sometimes dangerous, sometimes routine and sometimes—when they were successful—exceedingly rewarding.

"Why did you quit?" She was looking at him as if he was king of the hill, which he wasn't. Never pretended to be, but if she wanted to think so, then what the hell—who was he to disillusion her?

"I'd put in a lot of years. It was time to get out if I wanted to start another career. Besides, I'd discovered that, while I liked the work, I don't have a military personality."

She seemed to consider that for a while. She had a way of squinting off into the distance when she was thinking that made him wonder if she needed glasses.

Picturing her with a pair of horn-rims sliding down her minuscule nose, he grinned. They were cruising in a wide circle over the place where her husband's plane had gone down. On a clear day, with the sun directly overhead, you could see the dark shadow.

Kurt didn't see any reason to mention it. In fact, he didn't see any reason to hang around here any longer. The wind was kicking up. The *R&R* had a soft chine on her that cut through a choppy sea, but he'd just as soon not have a seasick woman on his hands again.

Or any woman at all, he reminded himself with a certain element of regret. At the moment he had a fourteen-year-old kid to look after, a determined child welfare worker he was doing his best to avoid, a new career to worry about, a house he was wanting to buy and enough experience to know that women were a lot like Diamond Shoals. Exciting. Beautiful to look at with their ice-green, lace-edged frills dancing in the sunlight against the deep royal blue of the Gulf Stream, as long as you remembered to keep a safe distance away.

Just like a lot of beautiful, innocent-looking women, those same beautiful, innocent-looking shoals had claimed more than their share of victims over the centuries.

They cruised in comfortable silence for a while. Deke took tiny sips from her glass. The bottle was still over half full. Now and then Kurt pointed out something of interest. Gulls diving for supper. Several charter boats trolling offshore. He told her the blue-fins were running, and she beamed another smile at him, looking pink-cheeked, pink-nosed and happier than she had all day.

Thinking smugly that Frog wasn't the only member of the crew with social skills, he began to hum a Beatles melody. Trouble was, it sounded, even to his tone-deaf ears, more like a bass fiddle being tuned.

But the sunset was great. Everything he had hoped for. Deke wanted to go below for her camera, and after cautioning her to hold on to the rails, Kurt let her go down alone. All his masculine instincts were urging him to pick her up and carry her wherever she needed to go, to wait on her hand and foot, to cushion her in cotton wool. Which was one reason he thought he'd better let her go alone. He couldn't remember the last time a woman had affected him this way. Had Dina? It had been so long, he couldn't recall. Evelyn sure as hell hadn't.

A long time ago, back in his high school days, he and his two best buddies had organized something called the 3-H Club. Hooch, Horsepower and Hormones. Which translated into beer, fast cars and women.

A couple of sips of champagne might qualify as hooch, and he had a pair of rebuilt Detroits that supplied more than enough horsepower, but when it came to women—

"Oh, look at that," cried the woman, who had just lurched onto the bridge again. Her camera case whacked him in his bum thigh just as her fist grabbed at his belt again. "Here, hold on to my case while I get out my light meter, would you, please?"

He would. If she'd asked him to pose with a petunia between his teeth, he probably would have done that, too. Fortunately, she had better taste in subject matter.

The sunset was a good one. Every shade of red, pink and orange was represented, with a wedge of gunmetal gray and a smudge of greenish blue at about three o'clock. Halfway through a thirty-six-exposure roll, a school of porpoise decided to escort them in past the bell buoy. Deke was ecstatic. Kurt beamed as if he'd personally arranged the show for her enjoyment.

Hell, he was enjoying it himself. Usually he just ran the boat, looking for enough action to satisfy a bunch of beered-up fishermen.

"Oh, I hate for it to end," Deke said with a sigh as he cut the power and glided in past the breakwater. Standing beside him, her brown hair blowing untidily around her face, her shirttail hanging over her trim black slacks, she came all the way up to his armpit. For such a small package, she packed one hell of a wallop, he thought with reluctant admiration.

A trio of gulls swooped hopefully over their wake, searching for scraps of leftover bait. The muffled throb of a wet exhaust vibrated sweetly through the soles of his deck shoes. On the whole, Kurt thought, it had been a pretty memorable charter.

Now it was time to start forgetting it and looking forward to the next one. Storm permitting.

Frog was waiting on the pier, eating peanuts and reading a comic book. He leapt to his feet and grabbed the line Kurt tossed him, his face flushing when he caught sight of Deke emerging from the cabin, struggling into the sweatshirt she'd discarded earlier.

"How'd it go?" he called out.

"Wonderful!" She spared another of her five-hundred-watt smiles. "We saw lots of porpoise and I almost saw a flying fish, and the sunset was really and truly spectacular."

Kurt grinned at that business about the flying fish. He'd told her about them, and she'd nearly popped a socket staring out over the water. If near misses counted, he'd *almost* seen her sprawled naked and waiting in his bunk instead of curled up there with a bucket in her arms.

Surprisingly enough, Frog was at his most charming. He usually turned it on only when he was hoping for a big tip, which was hardly the case where today's fare was concerned. He had a thing about women. A hard-boiled attitude that was discouraging to someone who was doing his damnedest to civilize the boy. Kurt had a feeling that his mother, whoever and wherever she was, had done a real number on him.

"Hey, you guys wanna go grab something to eat? I'm so hungry my gut's sucking wind."

"To put it politely," Kurt muttered. He hadn't figured on taking her out to dinner. He'd figured the sooner he wound up his business with Ms. Kiley, the better for all concerned. She was the kind of woman who came on slow and then struck like a force-five hurricane, and the last thing he needed at this point was another storm. He had a bad feeling about the latest tropical depression making its way west from Africa.

"Oh, I couldn't," Deke murmured.

"Sure you could. You gotta eat, don't you?" Frog hopped into the cockpit and handed her onto the wharf as if she were made of porcelain, leaving Kurt to shut down and finish tying up, things Frog was usually eager to do.

"You can swab 'er down and gas up after supper," he said.

"Aye, sir!" Frog's grin was a work of art, freckles, oversize teeth, ill-assorted features and all.

"You young scamp," Kurt grumbled fondly, watching as the two of them headed up the pier. Throwing a bowline over a cleat on the pier, he leapt up and followed along behind, watching the swish of Deke's tidy little stern, the way she swayed, bumping against Frog's skinny arm.

It occurred to him that not all the swaying was due to having been aboard a rolling boat all day. Some of it might be champagne-induced.

Ah, hell. He'd better drive her to wherever she was staying. As for dinner, he'd just as soon cut his losses and get out before he got in any deeper, but he had a feeling it wasn't going to be that easy.

Four

Kurt insisted on driving her to her motel, although Deke protested that she was perfectly capable of driving herself. Frog was on the verge of climbing into Deke's elderly car with them when a Jeep load of teenagers cruised past. He quickly backed off, pretended an interest in the ramshackle bulletin board that was covered with yellowed clippings and faded brochures, a look of utter boredom settling over his face.

"You're welcome to ride with us," Deke offered.

He shrugged a pair of wide, bony shoulders and said, "Ah, you guys go ahead. Meecha there, okay?"

"You might want to change your shirt first," Kurt suggested. "You've got about all the mileage you can get out of that one."

"Aw, man," the boy cried plaintively, "this is my best shirt."

If that was his best, Deke would hate to see his worst. She allowed Kurt to take her arm and escort her around to the passenger side. Somewhat to her surprise, even though they were back on solid dry land, she was still having trouble with her balance.

"You need a ring job," he told her as they pulled out of the marina parking lot and headed toward the town's only motel.

"I know. By the way, I'm staying at a place called Montrose's Motor Inn."

"I thought that might be the case." The town of Swan Inlet consisted of one motel, a general store, two churches, a few dozen scattered homes, eleven bait and tackle shops, a garage, a marina and three restaurants of the greasy spoon variety.

"Why do you call him Frog?"

"Who, Frog? Because that's what he calls himself. How long will it take you to get gussied up for dinner?"

"Do I have to gussy?"

"No, ma'am, not on my account. I only said that about Frog's shirt because I was afraid it might put you off your feed. Those stains are a whole season's collection."

"He's sweet."

"Don't ever let him hear you say so. He'll go out of his way to prove you're wrong. Sweet's not cool."

She chuckled, and Kurt felt it down to the soles of his feet. He wondered what it would take to make her feel the same sensation, and then decided maybe it was time he changed the subject. "Swan Inlet's premier dining establishment runs to a bottle of catsup, a bottle of Texas Pete and a can of evaporated milk on each table. If it's all the same to you, we'll pass up all that in favor of plastic plates, plastic forks and the world's best barbecue.''

"Will Frog know where to find us?''

"Sure. When he chooses supper, we eat burgers. When it's my turn to pick, we have barbecue.''

"Don't either one of you ever cook?''

"In case you hadn't noticed, our galley space is kind of limited. Basic, you might say.'' He unlocked the door to her unit, which was one of five, switched on a light, glanced inside and gave her the all clear. Gravely, she thanked him, stepped inside and closed the door.

Swan Inlet's crime rate was in the single digits, and usually fishing-tackle related, but caution was an ingrained habit for a man who had spent his entire adulthood moving from base to base, some of them in pretty rough areas. Besides, Deke was the kind of woman who invited a man's protection.

Fortunately, she was not, he thought with wry amusement as he lifted the hood of her car, one of those women who took a swing at any man who opened a door for her. What she was was...

What she was was here today and gone tomorrow.

And he'd damned well better not forget it.

She was quick as a minute. Kurt had just slammed the hood and was wiping a smudge of grease off with his handkerchief when she emerged, looking neat and feminine and surprisingly sexy in the same clothes she had worn all day.

"I only brought one change,'' she said apologetically.

"You look terrific,'' he said, and felt his face grow warm.

Damn. Thirty-eight years old, tough as boot soles, and all it takes to throw you for a loop is half a pint of female.

She wasn't even wearing makeup. Or if she was, it wasn't obvious. She still smelled of soap and shampoo, mingled with fresh salt air and what he figured might be hand lotion, since she'd come out rubbing her hands together.

"We can leave your car here and walk, if it's all right. It's not far. Couple of blocks, if we had blocks."

It was all right with Deke. In fact, it was just dandy. As small as it was, her hometown of Church Grove, Virginia, no longer lent itself to walking since they'd started cutting a new highway through less than two miles away. There'd been three unpleasant incidents in the past year alone.

They had gone only a few yards when she noticed Kurt's slightly uneven gait. What she had thought of earlier as a lack of sea legs evidently wasn't. She had a feeling it was something more than a pebble in his deck shoes, but it wasn't her place to ask. He was practically a stranger, after all.

Even if he didn't feel like a stranger.

That night Deke laughed more than she had laughed in years. The only other customers in the place were three teenage girls, the same ones, unless she was mistaken, who had driven past the marina in the pink Jeep. At the moment they were finding lots to whisper and giggle about, and Deke wondered if she'd ever been that young.

Frog, in a faded but almost clean sweatshirt, made a point of ignoring them. Atrocious grammar and all, he kept Deke entertained until the proprietor blinked the lights in a broad hint that it was nearing closing time.

Frog insisted on calling her Debranne, saying she "didn't look like no Deke" to him. Kurt finished his barbecue plate and leaned back against the varnished pine bench, arms crossed over his chest. He offered little in the way of conversation, but Deke was acutely aware of every flicker of his thick, sandy eyelashes.

The girls got up to leave. On their way out, they brushed past Kurt's table and self-consciously avoided looking at Frog, who just as self-consciously avoided looking at them. More giggling on their part. Scowling on Frog's. Deke wondered again if she had ever been so painfully young.

For no real reason at all she was touched. But then, it had been a strange day, all things considered. She didn't even feel like herself.

"Frog," she said brightly. "I told all my real names, the whole long list. It's your turn. I know you weren't christened Frog by your parents, so what is it really?"

His freckles paled as his face turned red. "Weren't christened a-tall, s'far's I know. Named fer m'old man, though."

"And his name was?" she prompted. She smiled at Kurt, expecting him to tease, to join in or at least to smile.

He didn't.

"Junior Smith," Frog muttered, and she couldn't bring herself to ask if he was Junior Smith, Junior, or Junior Junior Smith.

"I like Frog," she said thoughtfully. "Frog's nice. It has a certain . . . ring to it."

"Yeah. It's better'n what some kids call me," he mumbled, and Deke immediately bristled. She was on the verge of demanding to know just who had called him what, but Kurt took her arm and led her outside.

"Turning cold," he observed. "We'd better get you home."

But they didn't seem all that eager to get rid of her, and Deke wasn't at all eager to be gotten rid of. After tonight, she would never see either of her new friends again, and that suddenly struck her as a real loss.

There were no sidewalks. The combination of ancient oak roots snaking out into the path and a lack of streetlights made walking rather hazardous, but there was little traffic. Evidently, not much went on in Swan Inlet after dark.

"Nice moon coming up," Kurt observed laconically.

"High tide," Frog said.

"Rain on the way. I give it about a day and a half."

"More like two," said Frog, in what Deke surmised was an ongoing competition between the pair of watermen. She savored the warmth of two male bodies beside her, and the prosaic conversation. If either one of them had suggested strolling down to the marina to watch the moon rise over the water, she would have jumped at the chance. For reasons she didn't even try to understand, what should have been the most miserable night of her life, after learning of her late husband's infidelities, was turning out to be one of the nicest.

Three abreast, arms linked together, they strolled into the ghoulish light cast by the motel's green and blue neon sign. "You ever get down this way again, Miss Debranne, me'n Kurt'll take you out after billfish. Won't cost you nothin' but gas money, neither, right, Cap'n?" The boy shot a cocky grin at his employer. "Man, I'd like to see you on the other end of a five hunnert pound blue!"

Deke would have liked to thank Kurt for a wonderful day and an even more wonderful evening, but Frog wouldn't hush up long enough. For some reason, even though the girls were no longer around to appreciate his social skills, he seemed determined to practice them.

More competition? Reminded of a documentary she'd seen recently about how young male apes challenged the dominant male of the group, she wondered if Kurt realized what was going on. The pair of them did seem to have a special relationship, even if she wasn't quite sure what it was.

Outside her door, Frog pumped her hand and reminded her again that she was welcome any time she could get away from her birds and babies. She had described her jobs—all three of them. Frog had been more interested in the birds than either the books or the babies.

Kurt smiled at her, and she thought, *This is it. Oh, my.*

"Guess this is goodbye, then," he said. "Drive carefully tomorrow, y'hear?" He looked as if he wanted to say something more. His gaze seemed to move over her face, and hers certainly moved over his.

What was there about the man that was so fascinating? Other than the fact that he was probably a hero many times over but too modest ever to admit it.

Other than the fact that he was the handsomest man she had ever seen, eye patch and all.

Other than the fact that being with him lent her a sense of security—no, more a sense of completeness. It was strange. They hadn't even talked together all that much, but she couldn't recall ever being quite so aware of a man. A tingling, alive-all-over, under-the-skin kind of awareness.

Long after she went to bed that night, Deke wondered what they would have talked about if the two of them had been alone. Maybe nothing. Pass the salt. More catsup? The weather.

She wondered if Kurt would have thought about kissing her good-night. It hadn't been a real date. Just a part of the service.

Still, she thought about what it would be like to feel his mouth on hers, which surprised her, because she'd never been the kind of woman who thought about that kind of thing. At least, not with strangers.

It had felt so easy, so comfortable, strolling arm in arm under all those massive live oak trees, past white frame houses set back in the shadows, most with either boats or tombstones in the front yard. Some with both.

It was that kind of a town, back behind all the sleek fiberglass cruisers and the rod-bristling 4x4s and the weekend fishing crowd. There was a sense of permanence about it that appealed to her. The same sort of permanence she had grown used to in her childhood, with Granna Anne and her great-aunts and the three-story house on Chesapeake Street.

So much for permanence.

* * *

Kurt held the small, leather-cased instrument in his left hand and swore softly. He'd just stepped out of the head and was ready to turn in when he happened to see it under the shirt and cap Frog had tossed down when he'd come in from school.

It was too late to go out again now. She'd be asleep. Besides, if she was smart, she wouldn't open her motel door in the middle of the night in a strange town.

Tomorrow, he thought. First thing. He didn't have a charter, but he'd set the clock early.

Frog was already snoring in the other bunk, long limbs sprawled out in all directions. They needed more space before the kid did much more growing. Kurt was used to close quarters. Coast Guard billets weren't exactly known for their spaciousness, but a growing boy—a kid whose idea of security was having everything he possessed in plain view and within easy reach at all times—needed more space.

At oh-eight-hundred hours, Kurt jogged out of the marina parking lot, freshly shaved and dressed in his best khakis. He hadn't eaten breakfast—figured he might as well top off his last charter by taking his passenger out for pancakes at Joe's. He'd left Frog sprawled on his belly on the bunk, one big foot hanging off the end, one long, lanky arm dangling to the deck. It was Saturday. The kid could sleep an extra hour before they started putting the rebuilt engine in the truck.

She was already gone. He knew it before he even knocked on her door, but he knocked all the same. Her car was missing from the slot in front of her unit, but just in case, he dropped by the office.

"Checked out about five. Nice woman. Car needs a ring job."

"Yeah, I know," Kurt muttered distractedly. "She leave a forwarding address?"

"Nope. License number. I pegged her for Tidewater, Virginia, from her accent."

Kurt nodded and left the cramped office. He still had her reservation letter. Somewhere. If Frog hadn't tossed it out with the garbage. There were unseen hazards to trying to teach the kid to clean up his act.

That evening he was invited out to dinner. The blonde in the sagging halter, whose name was Ashli— "That's Ashli with an *i,* not a *y,*" had a hibachi on deck and was doing something to shrimp and pineapple, a cooking fork in one hand, a wineglass in the other.

"That's real nice of you, uh, Ashli, but—"

"Leonard's over on that Hatteras-55 that just pulled in this morning. He'll be playing poker all night, and I just *hate* card games. They bore me silly."

Kurt had a pretty good idea what kind of games she enjoyed. He wasn't interested. Funny thing— another time he might have taken her up on the challenge. "Thanks, but Frog's gone out for cheeseburgers. I've got to drill him for a math test on Monday."

"Gawd," she said, rolling her eyes. She turned her back on him and jabbed at a shrimp. Kurt had to admit, it was a pretty nice back. He was half-tempted to change his mind, but then, math *was* important.

Five days later the rain slacked up just as a yellow 1983 Lincoln with a peeling vinyl top pulled into the marina parking lot. He glanced up from what he was doing.

Down, boy. There's got to be at least a couple thousand of those old babies around these parts.

Carefully, he replaced the snarl of monofilament leader in the tackle locker and stood up. The car door swung open, and a pair of red sneakers dropped into view. Kurt started grinning. He dusted his hands off on the seat of his pants and adjusted the knot of his eye patch.

"You didn't have to come all this way for your meter," he said when she was halfway out the pier, her slicker glistening under the greenish pier light that had come on with the early darkness. "I kept waiting for you to call and tell me where to send it."

"I wasn't sure if I'd even left it here."

They were both grinning like it was a big joke or something, running into each other this way. Deke leaned over the boat and Kurt reached up and swung her aboard as easily as if the movement had been choreographed.

He'd forgotten just how small she was. And how feminine. She wasn't exactly pretty—hers was more the kind of beauty he'd seen once in an exhibit of black-and-white photographs. The kind of beauty that had nothing to do with age or wrinkles or fancy makeup.

"Here, get under the overhang, it's still drizzling. Want some coffee?"

"No, thanks. How's Frog?"

"Fine. He's off on a basketball trip to Raleigh this weekend. With the weather closing in, he figured he might as well go, since he wasn't going to be earning any tips. Besides, I think a certain twelfth grader who drives a pink Jeep is going.''

"Didn't you say he was only fourteen?''

"Yeah, well . . . I didn't say he had real good sense, did I? He's learning, but these things take time.''

"I'd forgotten how awkward it is, growing up.''

"You'll make it one of these days. Just hang in there.'' He grinned again. Lately he seemed to be doing a lot of that.

"I'm twenty-seven,'' she informed him.

"You've got plenty of time.''

Kurt was going on thirty-eight. He ought to have better sense than to be thinking what he was thinking. Hell, he was no better than Frog when it came to playing out of his league. Worse, in fact. He was old enough to know better.

And then neither one of them could think of anything to say. Deke touched the rats' nest of fishing tackle that was lying in one of the chairs. Kurt adjusted the tie of his eye patch again. Mostly he forgot he even wore the thing, but every once in a while, he became self-conscious about it.

With his one good eye he studied her the way he would study the surface of the water, searching for signs of fish. For the reddish shadow that indicated a school of drum. The choppy oil slick of feeding blues.

What had made her drive all the way down from Virginia when a phone call would've accomplished the same thing?

"I was afraid you'd be out with a charter today,'' she said, sounding a little shy, a bit embarrassed. He wondered if that self-assertiveness course she had told him about had struck again. This was not exactly a good time to be visiting the coast.

"A charter? Oh, yeah—we were booked up, but we had a couple of cancellations. Weather doesn't sound too promising for the next few days."

"Don't the fish bite when it rains? Mercy, how can they tell the difference?"

Kurt caught a faint drift of soap, shampoo and sun-warmed corn tassels. Perfume or just clean, wholesome woman, the stuff really packed a wallop.

"Matter of fact, I think we might be in for more than just a few showers. According to the last update, TD-11 just turned into Tropical Storm Irene. She's headed north-northwest, picking up speed and strength, expected to make landfall somewhere in south Georgia if she holds to her present course."

Deke sat down rather suddenly on the fighting chair that wasn't filled with a tangle of fishing tackle. "I might have known something else would happen." She managed a bleak little smile. "Once I'm satisfied that things are about as bad as they can get, they get worse. Either that or I screw up. I seem to have a real talent for it."

So then she had to explain about the day-care center being shut down until further notice due to an outbreak of *E. coli,* and about the vacate-premises notice she had received in the mail just yesterday, telling her she had three weeks to find another place to live and move out.

"Is that legal?" she asked plaintively. "I mean, can they actually do that? I thought a person was entitled to at least six months' notice."

She gazed up at where Kurt, leaning against a stanchion, smiled at her, looking tanned and handsome and slightly piratical except for his remarkably gentle gray eye. "I'm no expert," he said, "but I think six months' notice is somewhat excessive. Did you ask your super about it?''

"He says the lease says six weeks, but that doesn't count when it has something to do with safety violations. All I know is that I'm going to have to find a place to stay and then pay to get moved, and with one of my jobs gone and the advance on the proposal I just sent in not expected for at least six weeks, I'm just—I'm royally pi—*peed!*''

Kurt threw back his head and roared.

As for Deke, she couldn't have looked more mortified if she'd wandered into a tea party strip, stark naked.

"Miffed, is what I meant to say. It's that blasted course I took that was supposed to teach me to stand up for my rights instead of just lying there like a worn-out doormat. I think I must have missed a few installments.''

Kurt took out a handkerchief and blotted his good eye. "Why don't we talk about it over supper? You can't head back on an empty—'' He broke off as a burst of static came over the radio. "Hang on a minute, will you? This might be important.''

Turning, he fiddled with a coverless radio and frowned. Deke admired the long line of his backside, all the way from his broad shoulders right down to a pair of neat if somewhat hairy ankles. Even in late October, he didn't wear socks. Gray moccasin-type deck shoes and faded khakis. That was all she'd ever seen him wear, but she could easily imagine him in a pirate's costume. Or a Coast Guardsman's uniform.

Or nothing at all...

"She's picked up strength,'' he said, adjusting a knob that squelched the roar of static. "They're expecting her to make hurricane strength by daybreak tomorrow.''

''Oh, dear,'' she murmured.

''That about says it. Oh, dear.'' Then he grinned, and suddenly, the drizzle that had been falling all week, the potential hurricane and her personal problems seemed to fade into the mists. ''We'd better get a move on before the last eatery shuts down for the duration. Otherwise, it'll have to be cornflakes and chocolate milk.''

Which didn't sound quite as awful as it might. Deke suddenly realized that she was famished. And as long as it was already dark, what difference would another hour or so make?

She stood and reached for her purse, and Kurt smiled that lazy, devastating smile of his and said, ''Let me get some rain gear. We'll have to go in your car. Mine's in a borrowed garage. I got the engine back in, but now she needs a new flywheel.''

''That's all right,'' she said breathlessly, and truly, it was. If he'd asked her to swim to the nearest restaurant, she would have peeled off her shoes and jumped in without a second thought. Which didn't say a whole lot about her ability to learn from experience.

''I'll need to start back by nine,'' she said, trying to sound firm and levelheaded.

''No way. You can't drive all day and then turn around and drive back in the rain after dark. Stay overnight and head back tomorrow.''

''I wish I could, but I just can't,'' she said wistfully.

"Why not? The motel's probably empty. I bet old Montrose would even let you have the presidential suite."

"You mean the one with two towels instead of just the one?" She laughed, but it was a halfhearted effort. "Kurt, I just can't afford it, what with moving and all. The cost of moving my organ alone is horrendous."

"Then stay here. Frog's gone—you can have his bunk."

Moving her organ?

"Tell you what," he said before she could protest. "Let's go grab some supper and a few groceries and come back here and hash it out. If you want to use Frog's bunk, I'll sleep out here in the cockpit."

"Oh, I couldn't let you—"

"No problem. I sleep out here a lot. A bedroll, a can of mosquito repellent, and it's better than a two star hotel."

"But it's raining."

He shrugged. He could tell he was wearing her down. "So I'll sleep under the overhang. If the rain blows in, I'll improvise."

She sighed. "I really should go back tonight. I'm expected to feed thirty-seven baby birds in the morning."

"Who did it last weekend?"

"The owner. Biddy Cummings."

"Who'll do it if you break a leg and can't get there?"

"Probably one of the people who come in to play with the birds. There's lots of bird people who just enjoy being around them, and Biddy doesn't mind.

She says they need to be handled. The birds, not the people.''

Yes, and more than one of those volunteers had expressed an interest in her job. Jobs weren't all that plentiful in Church Grove. People who had them tended to hang onto them.

"Well, then, what's the big deal?"

The big deal was that she earned five dollars and twenty-five cents an hour less deductions when she was there. When she wasn't, she earned zip.

However, night driving, especially in the rain, had never been her favorite thing. "Are you sure Frog won't mind?" she asked tentatively.

So much for assertiveness.

Kurt couldn't suppress his grin. "Lady, he'll be heartbroken that he missed you, but he'll be honored as all get-out that you slept in his bunk. Believe me, you've gone and charmed the kid right out of his size thirteen cross trainers. Up until now he seemed to think women had to be cheerleaders or drive pink Jeeps to be good company."

He lifted her carefully onto the pier and then leapt up after her just as nimbly as if he hadn't lost a chunk of his left thigh to a piece of flying cowling a few years earlier.

Taking her arm in his, he hurried her down the pier to her car, feeling an edgy kind of excitement that had nothing at all to do with the weather and everything to do with the laughing woman jogging along at his side.

Five

To her list of things over which to feel guilty, Deke added the fact that she was as excited as a kid on Christmas morning at the thought of having Kurt all to herself for a few hours. With everything else she had on her mind—her jobs, her next book, finding a new home and then hiring movers who hadn't herniated themselves trying to carry her monstrous organ up two flights of stairs the first time—you'd think she would had have better sense.

And it wasn't because she didn't like Frog, because she really did, only being alone with Kurt Stryker was...

It was special. Because he made *her* feel special. Without even trying, he made her feel like someone she wasn't. Like a beautiful, exciting woman who had a functioning brain in her head and a few valid opinions to offer.

Mark had never been interested in her brain. He had liked the way she looked, with her upswept hair and her retro dresses and Granna's old-fashioned screw-back earrings and cameo. He'd called her his little Gibson Girl, but once the novelty wore off he had tried to change her into someone else. When that hadn't worked he had simply lost interest.

Kurt wasn't like that. At least, she didn't think he was. He asked questions and actually listened to the answers. He was even more handsome than Mark had been, in a weathered sort of way. But after the first hour or so she had forgotten the way he looked and grown increasingly aware of the quiet strength underneath all that masculine perfection.

Mercy, they had even laughed together! That was something she had never done with Mark, either. But then, Mark had never had a sense of humor, only she'd been too shy and inexperienced to notice until it was too late.

Deke told herself there was nothing particularly romantic about a rainy October night on the Carolina coast, but as long as she was there she was determined to savor every minute of it. Imagine, setting out on a three or four hour drive at two o'clock in the afternoon in the face of an impending storm.

Of course, she hadn't known about the storm. Or at least, how impending it really was. Nor did she want to know. Like Scarlett, she would think about that tomorrow.

Now she dutifully creamed her coffee from the can of evaporated milk on the table and found, somewhat to her surprise, that it wasn't too bad. They had come to the only restaurant that still remained open, the others having already nailed plywood over doors and windows and put out the Closed signs.

"What will you do?" she asked. "About getting ready, I mean."

"Tonight? Nothing much. Tomorrow I'll move the boat to a more protected mooring, make sure the batteries are charged, double-check the bilge pump and the switches—tighten down the nut on the stuffing box, check the cleats and bit for rusted bolts, check the chaffing gear..."

She blinked. "Oh. Is that all?"

Kurt looked thoughtful, and a thoughtful-looking Kurt Stryker was something to see. "Well...I reckon I'll take the radio and navigational gear out of the locker on the flying bridge—the thing leaks in a hard rain—and stow it below. Then I'd better check the weep holes—"

"Weep holes?"

"Drains in the deck hatches. Sometimes they get stopped up with fish scales and gunk."

"Oh. Of course."

"And then I reckon I'll go see who needs a hand getting plywood nailed up—the usual. Maybe lay in a few supplies."

"What if the storm turns around and goes back where it came from?"

He shrugged. "Then I guess we'll all count ourselves lucky."

Leaning against the high-backed bench, he looked every bit as relaxed as if both his home and his livelihood weren't in danger of being lost within the next thirty-six hours. It occurred to Deke that for a man of his background who had spent the last few years flying rescue missions, often under extreme weather conditions, this was probably nothing out of the ordinary.

She was interrupted in her musings by the proprietor, who stopped by their table with a message for Kurt. "Almost forgot—that woman was in here again today looking for you. Said she'd gone by the boat, but either you weren't there or you were layin' low."

"Damn." The word was spoken softly, which made it all the more effective. "She say anything else?"

"Nope. She'd already checked by the school and found out about the trip to Raleigh. Don't think she liked that too much, missing the boy and then missing you. Didn't look none too happy."

"Yeah, well—thanks, Joe."

"Anything I can do, just let me know."

Deke didn't know what the stuffing box Kurt had mentioned a few moments ago was, but if it had anything to do with human emotions, he had just tightened the nut down on his, real hard. Not a smidge of expression remained to be seen.

"Shall we?" he asked, rising and holding out a hand without even looking to see whether or not she was ready.

A whole swarm of second thoughts descended on her as they hurried out to the car in the blowing rain. "Kurt, I know you have a lot on your mind, so why don't I just drop you off and head on home tonight? I don't mind, honestly I don't."

He settled her into the passenger seat, then jogged around the hood and slipped in beside her. It occurred to her that there was more than a small streak of male chauvinism in the man, and yet it didn't bother her. Not much. Not yet, at least.

"No way," he said flatly. She could feel herself beginning to come to a simmer. Kurt started the engine and then just sat there, staring at the swinging sign that advertised Joe's Place Seafood And Etc.

Then he turned. In the dim reflected light, she tried hard to make out his expression. "Don't even think about it," he said flatly. "This is no time to be on the road, Debranne." Some of her steam began to evaporate. He was only showing concern. "There'll be a steady stream trying to beat tomorrow's evacuation traffic."

"Evacuation? Do you really think it will come to that?"

"Probably. All up and down the Banks, natives generally stay put—locals generally don't. Tourists never do. I don't want you on the highway tonight, so just humor me, will you?"

And then he shot down the last of her defenses by turning that slow grin her way. The warm twinkle in his one gray eye made it seem almost reasonable. He had so much on his mind, after all, and the last thing he needed was to have to worry about her running into trouble alone on the highway on a dark and stormy night. She put it down to all that rescue training.

Deke could have told him that her being alone, whether on the highway or anywhere else, was none of his business, but deliberate rudeness was not in her repertoire. So now she had one more worry to add to her list. Kurt Stryker. She was rapidly falling under his spell. He affected her physically, and Deke had never even been all that interested in the physical side of a relationship. Unlike several of her friends, she never even went out of her way to ogle the highway construction crew. Not that they were anything special, but boots, hard hats and bare chests seemed to turn some women on.

Khakis, deck shoes and an eye patch—now that was something else again.

So...some woman was running around town, leaving messages for him. A wife? An ex-wife or girlfriend? What if he was one of those deadbeat dads?

Not Kurt Stryker, she told herself, and then she told herself it was none of her business.

And then she heard herself ask, "Is there a problem?"

Kurt started to deny it, but then he shook his head. "Yeah. There's a problem."

"Can I help?"

They'd pulled onto the highway. In the dark interior of the car, she couldn't even make out his features, but when he reached over and laid one hand on her thigh she knew there was nothing the least bit sexual about it. "No, honey, this is my problem, but thanks for offering."

So that was that. They were casual friends, no more. Friends who were about to spend the night together in the cramped confines of a forty-eight-foot cabin cruiser, but that didn't give her any right to intrude on his personal life. He'd as good as said so.

Kurt pulled up as close to the pier as possible, and Deke reached into the back for her umbrella. She hadn't brought an overnight bag because she hadn't planned to stay overnight.

"Wind's picked up," Kurt observed as he hurried her along the pier. She was soaked from the knees down by the time he lifted her and swung her aboard.

Under the protection of the canopy, she shoved back the hood of her slicker. "At least it's not cold. I hate a cold rain, don't you?"

Although there'd been a time when she'd thought a cold rainy night would be wildly romantic. Two people curled up together in front of an open fire, listening to music, drinking wine, making sweet, leisurely love...

But rain, as it turned out, only made Mark impatient. It spoiled his plans. Rain or not, he'd been a go-into-Norfolk-and-do-the-towner, not a stay-home-and-make-lover.

Kurt followed her down into the salon that had been called, until the boat's recent reincarnation as a charter, a cabin. He took a clean T-shirt and a pair of white socks from a locker and held them out to her. "Will these do to sleep in?"

They would do wonderfully well, and she told him so, and then, to her delight, he produced one of those miniature toilet kits airlines offer when they've just canceled the last flight of the day and you find yourself stashed in a cheap hotel, sans luggage. It had happened to her only once, but she'd sworn to carry a toothbrush in her purse from that day forth, but of course, she hadn't.

"Semper paratus," he said with that crinkly smile that had such a crazy effect on her metabolism.

"Which means?"

"Always prepared. Coast Guard motto. Blankets and clean linens in the locker under your bunk. If you need anything else, just give a shout. I'll be right outside."

With the rain drumming down on the water, she doubted if he'd hear her if she shouted her head off, but she nodded and turned away, feeling both relieved and disappointed.

So. This is it, she thought.

Well, what did you expect, silly? A storybook romance? The pirate and the princess? The captain and the widow?

"Grow up," she muttered. Stepping into the compact bathroom that Stryker called a head, she sucked in her breath and managed to shut the sliding door.

Sometime before daylight, Deke woke up suddenly, aware of being in a strange place, hearing strange sounds and being practically paralyzed from sleeping on a mattress that was evidently stuffed with broken chunks of concrete. She had never been one of those hardy souls who insisted that sleeping on a miserable mattress was good for your body, your character and your spiritual well-being. As far as she was concerned, soft was good. Softer was even better.

"Wha'sa matter?" someone mumbled from a few feet away.

It took less than a minute to get her head together. She'd always been quick that way.

If in no other way.

She was aboard the *R&R,* and Kurt was in the other bunk. He was supposed to be sleeping outside on a bedroll in the rain.

Merciful heavens, she hadn't slept this close to Mark on the king-size bed they had shared—or at least, they'd shared it when he wasn't sharing his weekends with someone else.

"Something woke me up," she whispered.

"Prob'ly the halyard slapping the flagpole outside the marina office. Does that in a high wind. Sorry."

"No, I'm the one who's sorry. I woke you up. Go back to sleep."

"'S all right. Almost time to get up anyway."

She heard the sound of a yawn and it struck her as incredibly intimate, which was just one small sign that she'd better hit the road before she lost her perspective entirely. "I expect I'd better..."

"Yeah. Me, too. Why don't I start by making us a pot of coffee and checking out the latest weather bulletin?"

It was still drizzling. Deke had never really minded rain, but there was something unsettling about this particular rain. For one thing, it was doing weird things to her imagination. While Kurt was making coffee a few feet away, she slipped into the head and splashed water on her face, hoping to clear away the cobwebs.

Her eyes were puffy. They were always puffy when she didn't sleep well. That had been something else about her that had disgusted Mark. He'd told her there were creams for that sort of thing, and she'd bought one that had cost a fortune, only it had made her face break out.

"Hey, I found Frog's stash of cinnamon buns. They're probably no more than a week old," Kurt called through the thin door.

"Great! We can dunk them," she called back.

"Good girl," he said, and she felt as if she'd just been awarded a medal.

By ten o'clock that morning the rain had let up, but there was a different sound to the wind. A sort of

keening whine that made Deke feel not quite appre-
hensive, but certainly edgy. Kurt said it was only the
wind blowing through the outriggers, but she had her
own opinion. It was God, and he was trying to warn
her that she was asking for trouble again.

Besides, there weren't that many boats left in the
harbor with outriggers. Most of them had already
sailed.

"Wherever all the other boats went, shouldn't you
be going, too?" she asked.

"Nope."

"Well, then, shouldn't you go ashore, or at least
start doing all those things with weeping batteries and
stuffing nuts?"

"Yep."

"I need to get on the road," she said, and found
that she didn't want to leave at all.

"Wait'll traffic thins out some. Most folks left first
thing this morning. It'll take a few hours to get her
ready to leave."

"Will you evacuate then?"

"Nope. Truck's laid up."

She felt like screaming at him. There was a hurricane coming, for heaven's sake! What did it take to
shake him up? What if the boat sank with him on it?

Kurt lifted a bench seat and she saw several gallon
jugs. "Water," he said. And then he showed her a
supply of canned food, spare batteries, candles and a
first-aid kit that would have done credit to a small
clinic.

Deke was impressed. She knew he was trying to reassure her, not to impress her, but she'd been impressed the first time she'd ever laid eyes on the man,
and now that she knew him better, she was impressed

by more than his striking looks. As impressive as those were.

She had no choice. She couldn't just drive off and leave him here alone. Getting him to agree, however, might be another matter. "Kurt, I want to take you home with me."

Bent over a hatch in the floor—the deck, that was—he glanced over his shoulder and grinned. "Sure your mama'll let you keep me?"

"I'm not joking! I don't think you ought to stay around here. What if there's a tidal wave?"

"Storm surge? They say a rising tide lifts all boats."

"I'm serious! If the R&R sinks and you're on it, then what?"

"Honey, I do know how to swim. Believe it or not, guys with one eye don't really swim in circles."

He was touched by her concern, and he knew she was probably going to talk him into it. Hell, maybe that was what he'd had in mind all along. Not going home with her. He had no intention of getting all that cozy. But a weekend evacuation—a night or two spent together in an impersonal hotel room in a strange town where neither of them knew anyone else...

He wouldn't be the first man to take advantage of an evacuation notice. With all the excitement in the air, the situation had definite possibilities.

"What about Frog?" she asked.

"He's fine. I called while you were getting dressed. The game was last night, and they lost, but they're in high spirits, anyway. Coach said they'll stay put until they get an all clear."

They argued over a breakfast of hot coffee and stale buns. Kurt said that with half the population of the Banks evacuating, the route up the coast would be a mess, which was all the more reason for her not to tackle the trip home. It was pure malarkey, and Kurt had never been given to malarkey, but then he was in an unusually reckless mood.

"It'll take time to batten down," he said, as if he might be considering leaving with her.

"I'll help," she said promptly, making him feel like a real heel.

Kurt insisted on gassing up her car before the town's only service station closed down. Deke protested that she'd have had to buy gas anyway, but she might as well have saved her breath. Gentle the captain may be, but arguing with him was like trying to convince the tide not to rise.

She told him so, and then wondered why he laughed.

By noon, the rain had started again. The water had risen steadily until it was only a few inches below the top of the pier. Working as a team, they made ready to cast off. Kurt told her what to do and she stepped up onto the pier, untied the ropes—the lines, as he called them—as neatly as any sailor, then jumped back aboard.

"Hey, I'd make a pretty good mate, wouldn't I?" she called cheerfully over the noise of the rain, the wind and the muffled exhaust.

He sent her another one of those mystifying looks. Deke didn't even try to interpret it. Nothing at all that had happened since she had missed her light meter yesterday and come looking for it was turning out the way she'd expected it to. All she knew was that she had once more acted on impulse, and even though she might regret it tomorrow, for today she meant to savor every moment.

With the engines barely idling, Kurt positioned the *R&R* well behind one arm of the breakwater, away from the pier, between four free-standing mooring posts. He checked the chaffing gear on his lines and then tied her off, leaving enough slack to ride out the tide but not enough to knock against one of the pilings, patiently explaining it all just as if Deke might actually be considering a career as a mate.

Deke appreciated his patience. She appreciated his apparent unconcern as time passed and he calmly went about taking down the outriggers, moving his valuable instruments inside and checking to be sure his automatic bailer was working properly. She found out what a weep hole was and was not particularly impressed.

But as the sound of the nearby surf grew increasingly loud, she found herself wishing rather desperately that some of Kurt's sangfroid would rub off on her. Church Grove had been drenched by its share of passing hurricanes even though it was miles from the coast, but riding out a storm in a three-story house was one thing. Experiencing one aboard a small boat that was separated from the ocean by only a breakwater and a teensy little spit of land was another thing altogether.

"That about does it," Kurt said, casting a knowing eye around him and then hauling the dinghy up alongside.

Deke nodded just as calmly as if she couldn't practically feel the hurricane breathing down her neck. If there was one thing she was determined never again to be, it was a wimp.

Which was probably why she found herself agreeing, some five hours later, to sharing a motel room with him.

Didn't bat an eye.

But then, it was the eleventh one they'd tried. Hotels and motels. The first forty or so had had signs out saying they were all filled up, so they hadn't even stopped. She was almost sure Kurt had planned to stay with the boat, and she was so glad she had been able to talk him into coming with her, she didn't much care where they stayed. She, who couldn't swim worth a toot, would have stayed aboard the boat with him rather than leave him there alone, and she'd never been famous for her courage.

At least, not until she'd sent off for that dratted mail order course.

On the way out of town Kurt had driven her out to show her the house he was hoping to buy. In far worse shape than her own apartment house, which had recently been condemned, the poor old place looked so forlorn and exposed, perched on a marshy point of land, that she could only wonder at his judgment. Funny, he seemed so sensible, but then, everyone, she supposed, had a few hidden quirks.

They had to drive inland all the way to I-95 before they'd found a single vacancy, and then that was all it was—a single vacancy. In one of those fancy, Mediterranean-style places that was bound to cost a mint.

"Heavens, we could have been at my apartment before now if we'd driven north instead of west. Why on earth doesn't everyone simply go home?"

"Probably because most of them have rented cottages for the week, and they're not willing to forfeit the money on account of a couple of days' bad weather.''

Once they secured a room, they drove to the nearest mall to shop for a few essentials. Pajamas for Kurt, who claimed he'd never before owned a pair, and toilet articles and a change of clothes for Deke, including a flannel nightgown because she was inclined to be cold natured and she'd already discovered that Kurt was a fresh-air fiend.

''Guess what I forgot to bring,'' she said when they'd dumped out their purchases on one of the room's two beds.

Busy adjusting the temperature controls, Kurt glanced over his shoulder. ''Make a list of what else you need, and we can pick it up when we go out to eat.''

''My light meter,'' she said.

He stared at her for a second. ''Your *light meter?*''

Deke started to smile. Kurt started to chuckle, and then they were both laughing. Deke would be the first to admit that it wasn't all that funny, but laughter offered a safe relief valve for the tension that had been growing between them since shortly after they'd left Swan Inlet. Nor was it all on her side, although Kurt's tension, she told herself, was probably due more to worry than to sexual awareness.

''Kurt, do you think you ought to call Frog and let him know where we are?''

''Yeah, I'll do that.''

He prowled, examining everything in the room as if he were a tiger exploring a new cage. It occurred to Deke that this was just a cage of a different type. No bars, but certainly every bit as confining to a man who was essentially an outdoorsman.

His leg was bothering him, she could tell. After all the work involved in securing the *R&R*, he had driven the whole way. Claimed it helped him to think.

Deke hadn't especially wanted to think. Still didn't. Feeling ill at ease and determined to hide it, she sat on the foot of a bed, bounced to test the mattress, and said brightly, "Well. So far, so good. Now what?"

Kurt saw her grimace, watched the color rise to stain her cheeks. He knew she was uncomfortable with the situation—probably wondering just how she had come to be in this mess.

Well, hell—so was he. And not just because everything he owned stood to be wiped out before another day ended. And not just because social services was on his trail again. The woman had been on his case ever since she'd found out that Frog was only fourteen and was living under extremely unauthorized conditions.

He thought about Deke's careless words earlier that day, about being a good mate. Thought about them in a way he was pretty sure she hadn't intended.

Thought about them in a way that had nothing to do with the boy's needs and everything to do with his own. The truth was, he had been aware of her physically almost from the first. Not that that was any great surprise. He was male, after all, and she was an attractive woman. And when a man had gone without sex for as long as he had, it was only natural that he would be affected by certain things.

Like the scent of a woman's skin. The sound of her voice. The way the wind snatched up her hair and blew it across her face, and the way she laughed and tried to brush it back.

I mean, hell, he thought, watching her as she bent over to untie her sneakers, *what's a guy supposed to do when he's forced to spend two nights in a row with a beautiful woman? Study navigational charts?*

"Do you want to shower and change before we go out and hunt up some dinner?" he growled. He hadn't meant to growl, it just came out that way. Maybe because he was feeling predatory.

"If it's all the same to you, I'd rather get the going out done and then come back, shower, fall into bed and sleep for a week. I'm so tired I could drop where I stand, but then I'd wake up hungry in the middle of the night."

"Amen to that."

"To what?"

"I mean, yeah, me, too. About being hungry, that is. And tired."

But not the kind of hunger she was talking about. And not too tired to explore a few other possibilities before he fell asleep.

Maybe if he leveled with her. Maybe if he told her right up front that he was really attracted to her, and that, by the way, the county's child welfare agency had a thing against men taking in young boys to live with them, especially when they didn't live in a legitimate house, and that it had just occurred to him that if he had a wife, he might be able to make them back off.

He would never have considered marriage otherwise, not in a million years. Some lessons a man learned for keeps.

He could tell her right up front that, while he didn't love her, he really did like her. He enjoyed her company. He admired certain things about her and suspected he might admire a few more if he got to know her better, and that they'd both tried the other route and had the scars to prove it.

But that didn't mean he didn't want her sexually. He wanted her so damned much that about all he'd been able to think of for the last hundred miles or so was getting into her bloomers.

The truth was, he'd thought about it all week long, after he and Frog had walked her back to the motel last week. He'd been kicking himself in the butt for not kissing her. He'd wanted to, God knows, but not with a smart-mouth kid looking on and probably offering a running critique of his technique.

So the question was, would she be at all interested in marrying a stranger for the sake of a fourteen-year-old kid who had the table manners of a barbarian, a few questionable habits—a kid who outgrew or wore out everything he owned almost faster than it could be replaced, but who was bright and lovable and worth any amount of effort to salvage?

Not to mention the sake of a one-eyed, gimpy, thirty-eight-year-old ex-coastie who was barely treading water, financially speaking, but who had a hell of a case of the hots for a certain woman and was aching to do something about it.

Six

They must have eaten something, because she didn't have that same hollow feeling inside her that she'd felt earlier, but for the life of her, Deke couldn't remember what it was. Mostly because by the time they headed back to the motel, she had an altogether different kind of hollow feeling. This time it was her knees. And her head. And the space inside her stomach that seemed to be filled with fluttering butterflies, all trying desperately to escape.

They had talked at first—Kurt had told her more about Frog and about how the two of them had come to be together.

"You might say I inherited him when I bought the boat. I guess that makes us sort of like family."

She already knew Kurt's parents were both dead and that he had no brothers or sisters. She knew how that felt, too, because she was pretty much in the same boat herself. "Speaking of boats," she said, trying to ignore the way the timbre of his voice affected her nerve endings. "What do you suppose the storm's doing?"

"Gone out to sea, I hope. When we get back to the room, I'll tune in and find out."

When they got back to the *room*. The single *room*. Dominated by two big *beds*. The thought of those beds, no more than a few feet apart, ripped to shreds any possibility of polite dinner conversation. After a while, Kurt asked if she wanted any dessert, and she didn't. A little while later, after she had carefully folded her paper napkin and laid it across her plate, she asked if he needed anything else from the mall while they were out, and he said no.

Expecting to pay for her own dinner, she opened her wallet, but Kurt turned and said quietly, "Put it away."

"Oh, but it's not as if—"

In a voice as calm and even as if he were reading from the telephone book, he told her that he fully intended to pay all her expenses in exchange for her help with the boat that morning and the use of her car, and she might as well get used to it.

This time she got only as far as, "Oh, but—"

With one hand against her back, he directed her outside. Tight-lipped, they buckled themselves in and headed down the highway toward the motel. Deke was seething, and it wasn't entirely from anger.

It wasn't at all from anger, she admitted with a quiet sigh of defeat. Things were getting entirely too complicated. At the advanced age of twenty-seven, when any woman worth a grain of salt had learned to deal with a potential sexual situation without making a federal case of it, she hadn't a clue. Not a single clue.

At the motel, Kurt unlocked the door and switched on a light. Then they both spoke at once.

"If you want to shower first—" he said while she was saying something about the weather channel.

So Kurt switched on the TV and Deke grabbed the small basket of complimentary toiletries and then they sat, one on the foot of each quilted-chintz-covered bed, and watched the latest hurricane update. "Not as bad as it could have been," Kurt observed laconically, which proved that he, at least, had been listening.

Deke hadn't heard a word. She'd sat there staring at the screen like a zombie and missed the whole thing.

This is crazy! she told herself.

Tell me about it, self replied dolefully.

You don't even know this man. He could be a serial killer for all you know!

But then, all she'd known about Mark before she'd married him was that he dressed well, he hated cats, liked jazz, drove an expensive car and drank only imported wines.

And he'd been a great kisser.

She had never seen Kurt in anything but khakis. He was a beer man, not a wine man, but for the sake of a boy whose father had been a bully and a boozer, he'd admitted that he limited himself to one a day. As for his car or truck or whatever he drove when he wasn't driving a boat, she suspected it was in little better condition than her own. Worse. At least hers was still running.

He was a boatman who had been kind to a seasick woman while she was in shock after learning about her late husband's infidelities. A man who, to his credit, was trying his best to make a home for a needy boy.

As for his kissing abilities ...

She turned to look at him, only to discover that he was watching her. "Did you say something?" she croaked.

They were separated by approximately six feet of blue carpet, which should have been enough space to mute the effect he had on her circulatory system, but it wasn't. "This is silly," she muttered.

"You mean the fact that all either one of us can think of is what it would be like ... ?"

"What *what* would be like?" she snapped, and then felt the slow rise of heat sizzle all the way to the top of her scalp.

"What it would be like to make love," he said with that unflappable calmness that drove her up a wall.

And while she was still catching her breath from that, he said, "I'm going to kiss you, Debranne. I won't go any farther than you want me to, but if you have any objections to being kissed, I'd appreciate it if you'd say so now."

She caught her breath and even managed a gasp of laughter. "You mean like, speak now or forever hold your peace?"

He nodded gravely. "Something like that."

Neither one of them moved, but there were currents flowing around them. Oh, lordy, yes! And he was evidently as aware of those currents as she was, because for a calm, reliable sort of man—a man who looked so comfortable on the bridge of a boat—he was beginning to look remarkably *un*comfortable in the plush atmosphere of a luxury motel room.

Rising, he came to stand before her, his feet braced apart as if they were aboard the *R&R* on a wildly rolling sea. His fists were planted on his hips, and she thought if this was his notion of a romantic approach, then he had as much to learn as she did.

But then she noticed the smoldering look in his eye, a look that belied his seeming calmness. Taking heart from that, she searched for the words to tell him she was smoldering, too.

Stand up, you wimp! Meet him halfway! What are you waiting for—an equal rights amendment?

She was shy by nature, but she was working hard to overcome it. She was old-fashioned in some ways— a lot of ways—but she was working on that, too. Mark had swept her off her feet, and she'd been a perfectly willing victim, because it had been time. Past time.

Mark had certainly not asked her permission first. "Well, if you're going to do it, I wish you'd just…go ahead and do it," she grumbled, and to her intense embarrassment, Kurt threw back his head and laughed.

God, she was something! he thought. Instead of joining her on the bed, he reached down and pulled her to her feet. She barely came up to his shoulder. Being horizontal together would have been more convenient, but he didn't want to spook her. All he had in mind tonight was warming her up—a few kisses, nothing really heavy, just enough heat to start her to thinking about a relationship between them.

Then, on the way home tomorrow, he would spell out the parameters of that relationship. What he needed from it, what he could offer in return. Sex was important—in fact it was getting more important every minute he was with her—but at the moment, he needed her more for something else.

Forcefully reining in his physical desire, Kurt reminded himself that she was a widow with no family. A single woman who was being forced to pull up stakes and who was struggling to make a living with a couple of part-time jobs and whatever her writing brought in, which couldn't be much, considering she couldn't even afford a decent set of wheels.

What he was offering her was a fair deal. No more, no less. But then, whatever else he was, he had always considered himself a fair and honorable man.

Not to mention a man who was embarrassingly aroused and trying hard to ignore it. Nor was it only because he'd been a long time without a woman. He didn't want just any old woman, he wanted *this* one.

Steady as she goes, Captain. Come alongside gently now. Before she knows what you're about, you'll have her boarded, battened down, all systems secured.

He was still holding her in his arms. The bed was temptingly close. "Be still, woman," he growled when she started to squirm.

God, it was tempting—that bed. But his leg was hurting like the devil, and he had the beginning of a headache. There'd been a time, not too long ago, when a little pain wouldn't even have slowed him up. He must be getting old.

And she was too damned young, he reminded himself. Twenty-five? Twenty-three? She'd told him, but at the time it hadn't seemed important.

Now it did. He was damned near thirty-eight. She deserved someone her own age, someone who still had a few romantic ideals left. But then she looked at him with those big, innocent brown eyes, and he clean forgot about aching, aging body parts and lost ideals.

For someone so small, she was surprisingly strong. Her arms were wrapped around his waist, and her fingertips dug into his back as if she meant to hang on come hell or high water. The swift surge of possessiveness that swept over him left him shaken. There was no room for emotional involvement in the deal he had in mind. Sex, yes. Mutual benefit, sure.

But nothing of a deeper nature. He was no good at that sort of thing.

He watched her eyes grow darker. Saw the neediness there. She was as vulnerable as a day-old bird. Kurt knew he ought to back off, but he just couldn't make himself do it. And so he kissed her.

Her mouth was incredibly soft, her lips warm and faintly moist. She kissed with her mouth closed, and that in itself was a novelty. He savored her for a while—the taste and texture and warmth of her, and then he said, "Open your mouth for me, angel."

And she did. The sweet, spunky, soft, prickly little darling opened to him the way a flower opened to the sun, and all thought of any practical, mutually beneficial arrangement flew right out the window.

A long time later, he lifted his head and struggled to recapture his wits. She had her own unique taste. Kurt suspected it was a flavor to which he could easily become addicted. That might just become a problem, but it was a problem he would deal with when and if the need arose.

Right now, something else was arising, and dammit, he'd forgotten to stop by a drugstore!

So much for *Semper Paratus*.

Deke squirmed, trying desperately to get closer. He was crushing her against him, one big, hard palm flattened on her bottom, the other one stroking her back, and she had both arms wrapped as tightly as she could around his waist, but the fit wasn't quite right. Her legs were too short. She wanted to feel him against her where she ached the most. It had been such a long time since she had felt this heavy, hungry urgency.

And never, ever—not even on her honeymoon— had she felt like tearing off her clothes and having her way with a man.

"Whoa," he said softly, his deep voice coming from somewhere above her head. "We'd better slow down."

Slow down? Was this all there was? Why? Was there something wrong with her that turned men off once they got close to her?

Deke could have wept. First Mark, and now Kurt. And this time it hurt, it really did!

Of course, she was no great beauty. Never had been—never would be. She was allergic to most makeup, so usually she didn't bother. She was still wearing her old yellow sweatshirt and the same black slacks she had worn every time he'd seen her. As a fashion statement, it missed casual chic by a mile, and it didn't even have the advantage of being quaint and feminine.

Unfortunately, what was underneath was no better. Mark had bought her lots of fancy, lacy, frilly underwear that had irritated her skin. She'd worn it for as long as it had mattered, but once he'd lost interest she had gone back to her plain white cotton. At least it didn't itch.

Kurt said something under his breath. She thought it was a swear word. He looked as if he might have a headache. Something was certainly hurting him. He took his hand from her back, ran his fingers under the knotted tie at the back of his head and then jammed them under his belt.

She wanted his hand back where it had been. She wanted to reach up and untie his eye patch and soothe away the pain. She wanted to say, "Come lie with me and be my love," only she couldn't remember the rest of it—something about sharing all the pleasures.

But she didn't dare. Not unless she could make that darned mail-order course kick in. So instead she said, "I think I'm getting a headache," which was supposed to be his line, not hers. He was the one who'd suddenly lost interest, after all.

"Yeah, me, too. Must be the barometric pressure."

"That's bound to be it," she agreed eagerly. Too eagerly. "Wait right here—I've got something in my purse."

For a guy who'd just been let off the hook, Kurt felt remarkably unrelieved. His gaze took in her flushed face. There was a place on the side of her neck where his beard had scraped her delicate skin. Her hair, fine as cobwebs and the color of dry leaves, tumbled wildly about her face, as if she'd just woke up from a long, sex-filled night.

Watching her dart across the room to the fancy fake-French dresser, Kurt thought, *Judas priest, I'm losing my mind.* ''Deke—Debranne. Come back here.''

She looked up and blinked, one hand clutching a purse no bigger than a paperback book. She looked wary, and he could have kicked himself for what he was doing to her. With some idea of leveling with her—giving her a choice of making love now and marrying later, or making love and not marrying at all, he reached for her. The sharp movement put his leg in a bind, and it gave way unexpectedly, tumbling them onto the bed.

''Sorry.'' God, what a klutz. He was embarrassed, half-angry and still painfully aroused. ''It's been a long day,'' he muttered.

She wasn't trying to get away, but she wasn't trying to get any closer, either. The wary look in her eyes would have been enough to make him back off if it weren't for the damned bruised-rose-petal look of her mouth.

''Did you hurt yourself? Is it your leg?''

The TV was still droning on and on. Another front. Another tropical depression. Outside, it had started to rain as weather bands spun out from the center of the storm that had passed Swan Inlet at seventeen hundred hours and was drawing a bead on Cape Hatteras.

''Just a twinge. Muscle cramp. It'll be gone in a minute.''

It would be gone if he took off his pants and kneaded the muscles until they stopped spasming, but he wasn't about to do that. For one thing, he didn't want her seeing the mess that chunk of aluminum cowling had made of his thigh.

For another, he didn't trust himself in the same room with her without his pants on.

She held him the way a mother would hold a sick child. Actually crooned to him while she stroked his shoulder. And he let her do it, thinking that at the rate he was going, his love-making days might well be behind him.

With his jaw clenched against more than one type of pain, Kurt was tempted to tell her that that wasn't where her hands could do him the most good, but he didn't. Pain or no pain, it wouldn't take much to send him over the edge. His ego could do without that.

Reaching past his hip to his upper thigh, he dug the heel of his hand into the hardened muscle again and again, gritting his teeth against the pain. It took pain to cure pain.

There was a lesson in there somewhere, but at the moment, he was in no shape to go delving into any murky philosophical waters.

We make one hell of a pair, he thought with grim amusement, watching her struggling valiantly to stay awake. They were lying entwined on top of an acre or so of flowered bedspread. He'd set the room thermostat lower when they'd gone out to dinner. She had goose bumps on her arms, and he enveloped her in a bear hug, strictly for humanitarian purposes, he told himself, knowing it was a bald-faced lie.

The feel of two small bosoms pressing against his chest nearly finished him off. He eased a hand in between them and touched her there, and she opened her eyes and gave him a lazy-lidded smile.

"Mercy, I didn't realize I was so tired. Are you feeling any better?"

"Worse."

Her smile faltered. She looked so concerned he cursed himself for what he was about to do. "Debranne—sweetheart, I told you I wouldn't go any faster than you wanted to go, but unless you want to make love right now, one of us had better get off this bed. It's been a long day, and my resistance is shot to hell."

"Do you want to move?"

"Not particularly. I'm not sure I could if I tried."

"Well, I'm certainly not going anywhere," she said flatly. She was a gutsy lady, but it seemed to operate in fits and spurts.

It was all the encouragement Kurt needed. Slowly, hoping she didn't freeze before he could warm her up again, he eased her sweatshirt off her arms and tugged it over her head. Next he went to work on the button at the waist of her slacks. After that, it was short work to shuck her out of her panties and a scrap of a bra.

In the light of the single lamp, she was perfect. If her breasts had been twice as large or twice as small, she would still have been perfect. If her belly had been flatter or more rounded, she would still have been beautiful in his eyes.

A voice somewhere on the edges of his consciousness whispered that he was cruising in uncharted waters. He tuned it out.

"One of us is just a tad overdressed," she said, a thread of laughter in her voice.

It struck him—that hint of laughter—as the ultimate weapon. It was warm and sexual, inviting him to share far more than he was ready to share. Kurt wasn't used to women who could turn him on with laughter. It made him nervous. Wary. At the same time, it made him want far more than just her body.

He reached over and turned off the light before he removed his clothes. She protested softly that it wasn't fair, and he pretended not to hear her. Sooner or later, if all went as planned, she would have to see his scars. They weren't pretty, which was why he took pains to keep them covered. He told himself it was no different from seeing a woman without her makeup, or with her hair in rollers, or with blue mud plastered all over her face, but he'd just as soon she didn't see them. Not yet, anyway.

With one hand, he managed to get Debranne more or less under the covers, so that at least he could protect her from taking cold. Sliding in beside her, he felt a small hot hand on his chest, fingertips brushing over his nipples, causing them to harden instantly. He winced as the pressure in his loins increased and wondered how he was going to get through the night without disgracing himself.

With one last burst of sanity, he said, "I don't suppose...that is, some women take the pill for—Debranne, honey, I don't have anything t-t-to protect you, s-s-so—"

Oh, hell. He hadn't stuttered in nearly thirty years!

Her hands were all over him. He could feel the heat of her body reaching out to him. In desperation, he gathered her underneath him, unconsciously sparing her his full weight. It wasn't going to be easy, but after coming this far he was determined to make it good for her, if he had to stand under a cold shower for the rest of the night.

"You don't?" Her hands grew still. She sounded as if he'd just told her there was no Santa Claus.

"There's lots of ways—let me show you how—"

"But I want you, Kurt. I don't want *ways*. And I'd never hold you responsible—I mean, couldn't you just—"

He knew what she was getting at, but there was no way he could put himself inside her and not finish what he'd started. He had as much self-control as any man, but there were some sacrifices no woman should ask of a man.

Especially not a woman like Deke. Not of a man who had started visualizing her in his bed the first time he'd got a good whiff of her perfume, when she'd still been a grieving widow. Maybe even before that, when he'd watched her mincing down the pier in her flowered dress and her high-heeled shoes, with her hair pinned up on top of her head like she was on her way to the Queen's tea party.

She wriggled against him. One hand fluttered down his chest, over his abdomen, and he groaned. "Sweetheart, don't make this any harder than it has to be," he rasped.

Her eyes held all the innocence of Eve as she said, "I don't think I can make it any harder than it already is."

That tore it. Flat out tore it. Kurt rolled her over onto her back and slung one thigh—his good one—over her hips. "All ashore that's going ashore," he warned, and she laughed softly, caught a shivery little breath between her teeth and met him halfway.

And then he entered her. He tried to make it last, but there was no chance. It was give and take, surrender and victory all rolled into one. It might have taken billions of years to create the universe, but for Kurt, it all ended in one single fiery moment of glory.

He heard a shout and recognized it for his own voice, and was dimly surprised. He had never done that before. Shouted. Never allowed himself to lose control to that extent.

But then, he had never before known a woman like this one. For someone who admitted to being shy, she was gloriously, passionately uninhibited. He held her to him, their bodies damp and panting, and he wondered, half-amused, if it had anything to do with that course she had taken in self-assertiveness.

Because, God, had she evermore asserted herself!

He wanted more—suspected he might never get enough of her, but at the moment he wasn't up to it. His headache was gone, but the cramp in his leg was starting up again. It had had a real workout.

Next time, he might explore a few possibilities the missionaries had never even thought of.

"Deke?" he whispered. "Are you asleep?"

His only answer was a soft, satisfied purr. Feeling more relaxed than he could remember feeling in many a year, he turned her onto her side and gathered her up in the cradle of his body, where she slept till morning, her head on his shoulder, her bottom shoved snugly against his weary manhood and her small feet warm against his hairy shins.

Things had gotten out of order. He was an orderly person, never comfortable when things didn't go according to plan. They were going to have to talk, he told himself, and the sooner the better.

With what was left of his mental energy, he set out to compose a proposal, complete with addenda and disclaimers.

He never even got to the first disclaimer, the one about love not being a part of the bargain, before he was snoring softly. Sometime before dawn he woke up again. In her sleep, Deke had rolled over onto her side, and one of her knees had wedged itself between his thighs.

What happened next was as inevitable as the sunrise. Slowly, wordlessly, they made love all over again. If he lived to be a hundred years old, Kurt knew he would never forget the way she looked, her eyes soft and unfocused, her lips swollen from his kisses.

Seven

"**D**eke, I've got a proposition for you," Kurt muttered at the face in the mirror.

No, dammit, not a proposition, a proposal! the image retorted.

"Business proposition? Marriage proposal? Both?"

Whatever.

"Okay, here goes. Now it seems to me, Deke, that what you need—or rather, what I want is—"

What she needs—what you want—sort out your priorities, man!

Kurt scowled, one side of his face covered with lather as he tried to compose a brief, carefully worded proposal of marriage that could not possibly be construed as a declaration of love. He had examined his feelings and decided that genuine liking mixed with a hefty dose of lust was not too bad a basis for marriage. Especially considering the fact that so many marriages based on undying love ended up on the rocks.

Right. So he would start by pointing out that fact, and then he would say, "So you see, we're not talking romance here. You don't have to worry about that. All I'm looking for is a simple, straightforward, mutually beneficial arrangement."

Sure he was. His roof over her head, her body in his bed, and both their names on a marriage certificate. No big-deal romance. Just a piece of paper to keep the wolves away from the door.

He cleared his throat for a final rehearsal. "See, the thing is, I've got this little problem you might be able to help me with. There's this—"

"Did you say something?" Deke called through the bathroom door.

"Just clearing my throat!" Impatiently, Kurt reached over and turned on the shower again. "Where was I?" he muttered to the mirror. "Oh, yeah. The little problem. Y'see, the thing is, there's this nosy social worker who has a hang-up about placing kids with what she calls unsuitable parties, and lately, she's been giving me some grief. It just occurred to me that if I had a wife, I might stand a better chance of keeping Frog with me. I haven't had a lot of practice being a father, but I do know the kid would never make it in a regular foster home. He'd stick around about as long as it took him to stuff his pockets with food and any loose change lying around—although I think he's cured of that. Loose change, I mean."

Kurt shook his head. This wasn't going to work. All this talk about social workers was no way to court a lady.

On the other hand, he wasn't trying to court a lady. It wasn't her heart he was after, it was her signature on a marriage licence.

The sympathy card, man. Play the sympathy card!

He tried to look sober and responsible and less like a man who was having trouble keeping his mind focused on the main issue. "A boy like Frog..." A boy like Francis Junior Smith?

Nah... the kid had enough on him without spilling all his secrets. "You see, it's important for a boy like Frog to know you're going to be there for him even when he pulls some crazy stunt that makes you want to throw in the towel. I generally chew him out, but I make sure he knows I'm doing it because he's important to me, and I'm damn well not going to see him wasted. Mostly he's just testing to see how far he can go before I jerk him back in line, so I cut him some slack. I mean, a boy has to learn some way, but it's a dangerous world when you're walking that tightrope between man and boy. As tough as he is, in a lot of ways he's just a scared, lonesome kid, needy as hell and determined not to let it show."

The shower droned on. The mirror steamed up. Kurt swore and cleared a patch with his forearm. "Jeeze," he muttered. "How could any woman in her right mind refuse a proposal like that? Why not just cut to the chase, Stryker? Hey, Deke—for a nice woman, you really turn me on, so how about marrying me and my kid?"

Drawing the razor slowly down his left cheek, he tried to think of something he could say to persuade her. Otherwise, there was a good chance that a relationship it had taken him two years to build was going down the drain, and a new one that was coming to look more and more promising would be grounded before it ever took off.

But he had to level with her. No point in raising any false expectations. Then, no matter what she decided, neither one of them would be flying blind. None of this crying-in-his-beer-over-a-busted-heart business. He'd been there, done that.

And so, he suspected, had she.

After rinsing his razor, he put it away, stroked his cheeks appraisingly and reached for his eye patch. "Face it, man. You're not much of a bargain for any woman."

Aside from the age difference, he was a one-eyed gimp who might or might not still own a working boat. Who had plans to buy a house that might or might not still be standing. Who was hoping to be given custody, either formally or informally, for a fourteen-year-old kid with a foul mouth, an attitude problem, and holes the size of the Grand Canyon in his education.

The kid had liked her. She had liked him, too. Kurt had noticed that right off, because most women didn't. Frog was too old to be considered cute and too young to be considered interesting.

"Kurt, are you hibernating in there?" she called through the door. "Will there be any hot water left?"

Oh, boy. Running a comb through his damp hair, he checked his appearance in the steamy mirror one last time, then opened the bathroom door. "Sorry about that, but look, if you've got a minute, there's something I'd like to run by you."

She glanced up, her expression a startled mixture of guilt, embarrassment and apprehension. "Now, Kurt—if it's about last night, you don't have to say a word. I know—"

The shrill buzz of the telephone startled them both. Deke, who'd been folding the T-shirt she'd slept in, snatched up the instrument as if it were a life preserver. "It's Frog," she said after several seconds had passed. "He wants to know what I'm doing in your room."

By the time Kurt got on the line and had assured the boy that yes, they were both all right, and no, he hadn't heard anything yet about the *R&R*, and yes, they were damned well behaving themselves, and it was none of his business, anyway, Deke was standing beside the bathroom door, her feet bare, her face red, her fingers twisting.

"Did you have to say that? About behaving? He's probably guessed everything that—Kurt, is he all right?" She forgot her embarrassment in the face of his worried expression.

"Yeah, he's fine. They're leaving as soon as they round up all the strays." What made her think he wasn't telling her everything?

"Then it's all right to go back? Has anyone called to check on conditions?"

"Coach checked in with the Highway Patrol a couple of hours ago. Word is, things are pretty much under control, but power's still out over half the county. There's been some damage, but things aren't as bad as they could've been."

She told herself it was no wonder he looked worried. For all either of them knew, he could have lost everything he owned. *Some damage* could mean that some houses were flooded, some weren't. Some roofs were blown off, some weren't. Some boats were sunk, some weren't. Which wasn't particularly reassuring.

Deke tried to think of something comforting to say, but she was still feeling raw and exposed after jumping into bed with a man she hardly knew and making mad, passionate love. It was nothing dozens of her friends didn't do on a more or less regular basis, but she never had. Other than Mark, she had never had the courage. Never found a man who tempted her enough.

Until now.

Mumbling something about keeping fingers crossed, she snatched up a change of clothes and disappeared into the bathroom to shower.

Kurt paced, his deck shoes silent on the thick carpet. He rubbed the back of his neck, which had a crick in it from sleeping on a strange pillow. He rubbed the tense muscles of his left thigh, which were still protesting yesterday's hard work followed by the long drive. Followed by last night's calisthenics.

He made up his mind to put it to her on the way home. There would be plenty of time on the drive to Swan Inlet to explain the situation, sound her out about her own prospects and then lay his proposition before her. After all, part-time jobs could be found almost anywhere if someone really wanted to work. And a writer could write anywhere, couldn't she?

And besides, he was able to support a wife and kid. Not on any lavish scale with French champagne and a houseful of servants, but he could give her anything she needed within reason, including health care. That ought to count for something.

Yeah, right. Deke, darling, will you marry me and share my lust and be a mother to my semidelinquent kid in exchange for a roof, regular meals and whatever health insurance a veteran's spouse is entitled to?

Deke's hair was wet when she emerged from the bathroom. The motel's amenities didn't run to a hair dryer. She felt small and unattractive and embarrassed, and irritated because she felt all those things.

Kurt mentioned the need to buy gas on the way out, and she thought, oh, no—there goes another week's rent. And then she remembered that he'd insisted on paying all expenses, and that was even worse. A woman had her pride, after all.

"Are you hungry?"

She was famished, but she lacked the courage to admit it, knowing he was probably anxious to get home and survey the damage.

On the other hand, none of this wild expedition had been her idea. In fact, she didn't even know how she had come to be here. Right now she should be home in her own apartment, either looking over the classifieds for another place to live or curled up in her bed with her laptop struggling to make a three-page proposal sound like a potential best-seller.

"You want to know the truth? I'm starved!" she declared belligerently, daring him to make something of it.

He grinned that slow, crinkly grin that she found all but irresistible. "Yeah, me, too. Let's go find us a place that serves grits, hash browns, biscuits—the works, all right?"

How could a woman stay angry with a man who offered her both grits *and* hash browns?

* * *

It was just past noon when they reached Swan Inlet. Shortly after they'd left the restaurant and headed east, Kurt had started to say something, but Deke had rushed to distract him. She wasn't ready yet to talk about what had happened. What was the point in raking over yesterday's ashes? They had done it. There was no undoing it. She certainly didn't expect an apology, because it was as much her fault as his. What's more, she had enjoyed it every bit as much as he had. Not only the first time, which had been little short of cataclysmic because a woman who had once known sex did develop certain needs—but the other time, too.

The second time had been slow and sweet, almost dreamlike. They hadn't talked. Afterward, she had curled up in his arms and cried a little, for no real reason except that she hadn't cried in a long time, either.

Nor had they talked since. No more than "Did you lock the door?" "Did you get the key?" "Do you want more coffee?" and "Do you want to go to the bathroom before we hit the road?"

After that, whenever Kurt had tried to open a conversation, Deke had pretended to be asleep. Then, fifty miles or so back, they had started seeing storm damage, so they'd talked about that. Nothing major except where a small, storm-spawned tornado had touched down. Aside from the snapped-off trees and a section of rusty metal roofing twisted halfway around the top of a tall pine, it was mostly flooded fields and flattened crops.

Looking grim and preoccupied, Kurt drove directly to the marina. Neither of them had spoken a word for the last dozen miles. Tension had grown until all it would take was a single spark to set it off, and Deke wasn't about to supply that spark. It had dawned on her sometime during the drive that she might have fallen in love with him.

Oh, Lord, what if she had? What if she'd gone and done it again—fallen in love on the basis of one night of mind-boggling sex? Was that any better than falling in love with a man simply because she was flattered that he'd even noticed her?

No wonder she was having trouble with her third book. Her brains had turned to boiled eggs. *Soft*-boiled eggs! "I'd better start thinking about heading on home," she said tentatively.

Ignoring her, Kurt climbed stiffly out of the car and stepped up onto the wharf. Several of the boards were out of alignment, a few missing. Down at one end, a whole section had floated up and washed halfway across the parking lot.

Picking her way carefully, Deke joined him. "She's still afloat," he observed, sounding as calm as if it had never even crossed his mind that his boat might have sunk or washed out to sea or broken loose and been bashed against the shore.

Deke was beginning to think that the old saw about still waters described Kurt Stryker to a T.

Together they stood and gazed out over the placid water at the forty-eight-foot cabin cruiser floating peacefully in the center of her four mooring lines. Had it been only yesterday that they'd scrambled all over her, dismantling, lashing down, securing against the coming storm?

It just went to show how drastically the world could change in the blink of an eye.

"I seem to remember her as being taller," she murmured.

"Good memory," Kurt drawled, and she thought, what a dunce I am! Half of her is underwater!

After that, of course, there was no way she could leave. The bilge pump hadn't been able to keep up, and so there was pumping and bailing and Lord knows what else to be done, and he was limping again. The activity bus wasn't expected in until late in the afternoon, so the two of them—Kurt protested, but Deke insisted—rowed out to the *R&R* for a more complete damage inspection.

Kurt circled her slowly, checking for damage, his face expressionless. Not knowing what to expect, Deke was only relieved that there were no gaping holes in her sides. Her hull glistened like new snow in the brilliant sunlight, the bits of grass and seaweed plastered to her sides and deck only accenting her gleaming white paint.

Inside, there was water, but not as much as she had feared. Kurt rolled up the thin layer of damp carpet in the salon and pulled open a hatch to see if the batteries were still up. Deke began untying her shoes, peeling off her socks and rolling up the legs of the brand-new jeans she had bought at the mall near the motel.

They worked for hours. Late in the afternoon Frog hailed them from shore, and Kurt sent him foraging for food.

It was Deke who rowed ashore to collect the boy half an hour later. She was proud as punch to discover she could handle a pair of oars—after a fashion—without knocking herself out or falling overboard. With Kurt flat on his back, shirtless, surrounded by engine parts, it only made sense that she be the one to run any errands.

This is nice, she thought, *being a part of a team.* Her school had fielded a soccer team that had never once to her knowledge won a game, but Deke had not been allowed to play. She'd had severe asthma as a child, and as a result, she'd been so overprotected it was a wonder she'd been allowed to play solitaire.

Frog was sullen at first. He asked flat out what she was still doing there, and she told him about the crowded highway—which hadn't been all that crowded—and about Kurt's not having a vehicle to drive.

She asked about the game, and he shrugged and said nothing. And then she asked when school would be reopening, and he shrugged again. "Who cares?"

Frog did the rowing while Deke held on to the two grease-stained paper sacks and two gigantic paper cups of lukewarm cola. When she mentioned that whatever was in the bags felt cold, he told her they were damned lucky to get anything, because Joe's freezer had conked out on him and he was going to have to start dumping stuff as soon as he got the rest rooms baled out. "Man, you never seen such a mess! Water come up through the—"

"I can imagine," Deke said, and tried not to.

The meal was atrocious but surprisingly cheerful once Frog got over his sulks. They were all aware of how much worse things could have been. Deke dreaded leaving, but she couldn't put it off much longer. As it was, she might have forfeited her only remaining part-time job.

There were five cheeseburgers and two bags of cold, limp fries. Kurt divided the food. Frog glowered, but when Deke said half a burger and no fries, please, he settled down with one bony elbow on the table, devoured his third stale cheeseburger and started talking about cheerleaders and how close the team had come to winning the game and how he'd helped the driver fix a flat tire. "I might be a coach when I get out of school. Either that or a professional football player."

"Takes math," Kurt said, and Frog expressed his opinion of math in one crude word.

Kurt glared. Frog mumbled an apology, and Deke, feeling unneeded and unwanted, said, "I'd better get on the road." It was cold now that the sun had set. A damp kind of chill that leached into the bones. She'd left her sweatshirt somewhere—probably in the car—and now, wearing her new jeans and collecting her raincoat, she stood up and tried to think of some excuse to stay just a little longer.

If she'd been hoping for a polite protest, her hopes were quickly dashed.

Frog said, "You coming down again next weekend?" as if daring her to say she was.

It was hardly an invitation. She glanced at Kurt, but all he said was, "I'll row you ashore."

"When will you be able to go back and tie up at the pier?" she asked, her voice brittle with suppressed tears.

"A few days, if we're lucky. Depends. Lot of work to be done first. Some of the pilings need pumping down again."

He couldn't have sounded more impersonal if he'd been reporting on the weather. Blindly, she collected her purse and the plastic sack containing the clothes she'd worn yesterday. Rejecting Kurt's offer of help, she swung her legs over the coaming and dropped into the dinghy.

The thing rocked wildly for several seconds. Fortunately, she managed to sit down before she fell overboard. That would have left a lovely last impression!

While Kurt silently rowed the few dozen yards to the wharf, she studied the darkening landscape with every evidence of interest. She'd expected him to shove off the minute he'd set her ashore, but he didn't.

He walked her to her car, and she stood there awkwardly, trying to think of some polite and impersonal way to say goodbye to the man she had slept with, laughed with, shared silly little nuggets of information with—the man she very possibly had fallen in love with.

And would probably never see again.

"I guess this is goodbye, then," she said cheerfully. Dear God, how could he let her leave this way? "It's been a real, um—adventure."

He stared at her as if he were trying to memorize every detail of her appearance. Which, after all she had been through since she'd first arrived at Swan Inlet on Friday afternoon, she would just as soon he'd forget.

Her smile began to quiver and she turned away quickly, fumbling with the car door handle.

"Deke," he said quietly.

Tears broke through her lashes to leak down her cheeks. Oh, damn, hell and blast! "Look, tell Frog I said goodbye, will you? And good luck with his...whatever. Math."

"Deke, listen, I know you have to get on the road—you should have gone sooner. There's no place to stay, and I can't promise you—"

She glared at him over her shoulder. "Did I ask you for a single promise?"

"No, you didn't, but I'm not talking about that. I mean, about what you think I'm talking about. Yeah, well . . . maybe I am, but that's not what I'm talking about now."

He broke off, swore and muttered something about losing it, but by then Deke had had all she could take. She struggled with the door latch, which was tricky and had to be jerked and twisted at the same time. "Good luck, Kurt. Lots of charters and—and smooth sailing, and all that."

"Deke, wait. Dammit, now you're upset, aren't you? I never meant to make you cry."

Keys in hand, she yanked at the door latch. It gave way, and she flung a look over her shoulder that was supposed to be coolly haughty but probably missed it by a country mile. "You? Make me cry? Mercy, but you boat captains do have a superiority complex, don't you?"

He swore again then, using words that would have made her great-aunts rise up from their graves. And then he snatched her back against his chest, turned her in his arms and proceeded to kiss the living daylights out of her.

One of her feet was standing in a puddle of water. She never even noticed. The plastic bag containing her change of clothing fell to the ground. She never noticed that, either.

All she noticed was the blinding wonder of being held hard in his arms, of feeling his mouth on hers—of soaking in the heat and the scent and the taste of him, and wanting more.

And knowing it wasn't going to happen.

Eight

They had it out as soon as Kurt got back to the boat. Frog was rummaging in a locker, looking for his week-old cinnamon buns, when Kurt lit into him. "Would you like to tell me what that was all about?"

"Hey, get off my case, man. You wanna bring your bimbos aboard, it ain't no skin off my—"

Kurt held onto his temper—just barely. He'd seldom been driven to violence, and never with a child, but he was feeling raw and frustrated on several counts, and Frog was openly spoiling for a fight. Skinny, rebellious, with a chip the size of a redwood on his bony shoulder, the boy was ready to take on all comers.

"You're jealous," Kurt said slowly as realization dawned. "Oh, hell, son, you don't—"

"Man, you're crazy. And I ain't your son, and I sure ain't jealous of no dumb girl."

Ignoring the protest, Kurt said, "So that's it. You thought that just because I—"

"I didn't think nothin'!"

The gauntlet down, they confronted each other other across the space of a tiny, cluttered salon that reeked of diesel oil, salt water, marsh mud and stale fries. Kurt was torn between wanting to comfort and reassure the boy and wanting to shake some sense into his thick skull. He felt like taking a swing at something, but not at Frog. Never at him.

This wasn't even about Frog. It was the woman who was at the root of both their problems. The same woman who, only a few hours ago, he'd thought might just be the answer to all their problems.

Hell, he'd never even got to tell her. Or rather, to ask her. There'd been too much to do, and then the kid had rolled in with a couple of bags of throwaway food and a lousy attitude, and Kurt had started wondering where the dickens he could put her, even if she agreed to marry him. There was barely enough room for two aboard the *R&R,* and for all he knew, the house he'd been planning to buy had been trashed in the storm.

"Hey, you wanna roll in the sack, I'm cool," Frog said with a sophistication that was about as thick as the layer of gold on a two-dollar wedding band. "I'll get outta your way. Man, I was getting freaked anyhow, doin' all this math and readin' and dumb stuff like that."

With one forearm, Kurt took a savage swipe at the headache that was beginning to hammer at him. "Aw, jeeze. Look, that has nothing to do with it. Dammit, Frog, I thought you *liked* her!"

Frog shrugged nonchalantly, but his eyes told another story. "I was fixin' to move on, anyways. It's borin' here, you know what I mean? Nothin' but stinkin' old fish 'n' homework. No cable, nothin' but a bunch o' dumb girls who don't do nuthin' but giggle and poke out their ti—"

Kurt cleared his throat. Man talk was one thing. Crudeness was another. He'd thought they'd agreed on that point.

"I mean, hangin' in one place too long, man, it ain't healthy."

"Deke liked you. At least she did until you started acting like a jerk. She told me what a great kid she thought you were."

Frog rolled his eyes and fingered a crumb of salt off an empty French fry sack. Kurt gave up. "Look, before it gets any darker, I'm going to row over and check out the pier. You want to come along?" It was an out, if the kid had sense enough to take it.

He did. "Yeah, I guess. If they gotta tear all that old stuff out an' pump them pilings down again, we're gonna be S.O.L."

Kurt grimaced. "Don't push it, boy."

Frog smirked. "What, you don't know what it means? It means out o' luck, tha's all."

"Sure it does. Now let's get going before it gets too dark to see anything."

"O. L. Outta luck. Ever'body knows that."

What Kurt knew was that the boy wouldn't quit until he'd had his fun. He figured he might as well play it out before he launched into his standard let's-clean-up-our-act routine. "S.O.L.?"

Even tired, ticked off and frustrated on several levels, it was all he could do to keep from laughing at the look of injured innocence that came over the boy's face. "Certainly outta luck, tha's all. Whadja think it meant?"

"Do they still teach spelling in the ninth grade? Never mind."

Frog grinned knowingly. Kurt reached for the baseball cap hanging on the bulkhead, slapped it on the boy's head, and Frog readjusted it so that the bill shadowed the back of his bony neck. Torn between irritation and affection, Kurt wondered if he had ever been such a trial to his parents.

Yeah. He had. "C'mon, smart mouth. While we're at it, we'll see if we can borrow Joe's truck and ride out and look at the house."

"Sheesh. Like I care about that ol' heap, or somethin'."

"Yeah, like you care or something," said Kurt, who recognized the sound of whistling in the dark when he heard it. "C'mon, I'd like to check out the Detroits before we turn in, too, and I'll need a hand."

Deke sat on the organ stool and stared at her image in one of several mirrors that were a part of the ornate superstructure. Too bad Halloween was over. She could have passed as a ghost.

What she needed was a brand-new lipstick. Preferably Day-Glow red, if they made it in hypoallergenic. And maybe some blusher. What she didn't need was eye shadow. The shadows around her eyes were already the color of mildew.

"Well, Ms. Kiley," she whispered, "you've gone and done it this time. Stepped right smack dab in the middle of a big one."

Deke had been home for several hours, and home was even more depressing than she'd remembered. It wasn't only the dismal green walls that no tenant was allowed to paint over without written permission, plus a sworn promise to repaint them in the same bilious shade before she moved out.

It wasn't even the fact that her dolphin story was going nowhere. She was stale. Her ideas were stale. The dolphin idea had been done and done and then done again. What she needed was a whole new approach, only how could she think of little boys and dolphins when she was too busy thinking about big boys and—

Well. She'd simply have to try harder, that was all. Meanwhile, she needed to get serious about finding a place to live, preferably something on the ground floor. Preferably something with room for more than a coffeepot and a bed.

Oh, yes, and preferably something she could afford.

Then all she'd have to worry about was finding a mover who could handle her organ, and coming up with a brilliant premise for a story that wouldn't bore the socks off your average eight-year-old, in case it ever made it past an editor's desk.

"Darn it, Kurt, why did you have to go and ruin my concentration?" she whispered plaintively. "What did I ever do to you?"

Kurt stepped outside the real estate office and rammed the sheaf of papers into his pocket. Holy Hannah, he'd done it! It had damn near sucked his savings account dry, but he was now the proud owner of the ugliest house on the eastern seaboard. Perched on four and a half acres that was either bureaucratically protected wetland or valuable waterfront, depending on whether you were buying or selling.

All he needed before they could move in was a new roof, a new heating system, several new windows, new front steps, a new septic tank, new wiring, new plumbing and half a dozen different kinds of inspections.

Not to mention the basic appliances.

Not to mention a few coats of paint, both inside and out.

Not to mention a couple of beds, a table and a few chairs.

And that was just for starters.

Kurt told himself he'd got a bargain. "Hell, the old dump is about to be condemned, we both know that. It'd take a fortune to bring it up to standard," he'd told the agent.

"The property alone is worth more than the asking price. You know what waterfront property brings these days. They're not making any more of it."

"Waterfront, hell—the place is a marsh. I'll be lucky if I'm not locked up for trespassing on protected wetlands."

"There's plenty of high ground there." The agent had put on his glasses, no doubt, Kurt thought, to hide the gleam in his beady little eyes.

"Sure there is," he scoffed. "Almost three square yards that's close to four and a half inches above sea level, and we both know the house is going to cave in any day now."

"What, heart pine and juniper with cypress underpinnings? That place has been standing for nearly seventy-five years."

"That's what I'm saying. It's a dump. I'm crazy for even thinking about buying it, but I need a place to tie up my boat. If I can get permission to dredge a channel..."

They'd gone a few more rounds, but in the end, Kurt had signed on the dotted line, just as the agent had known he would. He wanted the place so bad he could taste it.

No, dammit, he *needed* it. If he was going to ask a woman to marry him, he had to have someplace to bring her.

"Man, you are crazy, you know that?" Frog was back at the pickup after a run to the nearest fast-food place. They seldom came to town, but now that the truck was fresh out of the shop with a newly rebuilt engine, they'd lit out first thing this morning for the county seat to buy some winter clothes and a new pair of boots for Frog, a six-volt battery and a set of jumper cables to replace those lost in the storm—and a house.

"Your boots still feel okay?"

"Yeah, they're okay. Uh...thanks. For the stuff an' all."

We're coming along nicely, Kurt thought, suppressing a grin. An unsolicited thanks and not a single four-letter word beginning with F or S. "You've earned it."

They headed toward Swan Inlet, the camper loaded with groceries that consisted mostly of potato chips, peanuts, store-bought sweets and canned drinks. Kurt had insisted on buying some apples and bananas and a gallon of milk, too. One of these days he was going to have to get serious about this business of nutrition, but not when he was under a load of stress. At a time like that, a man needed his full ration of empty calories.

After a while, Frog said, "I still don't know what you want with a house, though. It's a real dump, man. You wanna know what I think? I think we oughta 'doze the house, dredge us out a bunch of slots an' a good channel an' build us our own marina. We could put us a franchise burger place where the house is, an' a bait an' tackle place right on the wharf. Betcha we could get twice what old Etheleen charges for moorin', power and all that junk."

Kurt downshifted and passed a church bus on the narrow two-lane highway. "Which one are you planning on managing, the fast-food place or the bait and tackle?"

"Me, I figure I can make more in tips on board the boat, but when we don't have no charter, I could manage 'em both. Or you could run one an' I could run the other. Hey, whatever you want, man—I'm cool."

"Remind me to sign you up for a business course after you graduate from high school."

Which brought on the usual "Aw, man!" Plus a few remarks that translated roughly to a comparison of the leading-edge wisdom of youth to the cast-in-concrete stupidity of age.

On the whole, Kurt was encouraged. At least the kid seemed to be considering hanging around for a few more years.

Three weeks passed. They had four charters and found enough big stripers, yellowfin tuna and wahoo to ensure Frog some substantial tips and Kurt a few repeat charters. Life was good.

Life was lousy. Oh, sure, Oyster Point was swarming with carpenters, plumbers, electricians and their ilk, but every time he worked up his courage to place a call, either Deke was out or something came up and he didn't get back to the phone booth until too late to call.

Kurt knew damn well he was manufacturing excuses by the bushel. He told himself that what he ought to do was put it to her in a letter. Spell out his situation, his prospects, lay out his proposition and wait for her decision.

And wait. And wait. And sweat a little blood while he was waiting for her to make up her mind. And sweat a little more wondering if she'd even got the letter. For all he knew, the letter might fall out of a mail pouch and get chewed up by a dog in lieu of the postman's leg.

Or maybe she'd get it and trash it without even opening the envelope. The way he'd left her—the way she'd gone tearing out of the parking lot, spraying what little gravel the tide hadn't carried off...

Kurt swore a little and sweated a lot, despite the weather that had turned cold. He took apart his bilge pump for the third time, and it still wasn't working right. He'd evidently lost his touch.

Or his concentration.

Frog passed his English test—barely—and aced the math test. To celebrate, Kurt sprang for the CD player the kid had been wanting, thinking he might enjoy a little Haggard and Jennings, himself.

Instead, he got hard rock. *Loud* hard rock.

He wondered what kind of music Deke liked. She'd said she had an organ. He'd never even heard one outside a church. She hadn't struck him as particularly religious, but then, you never could tell about things like that.

God, he missed her. The day after she'd left, he'd found her yellow sweatshirt hanging behind the door to the head. It had her scent—sort of soapy and warm and corn-tasselly. Two days later, rummaging through the locker where he'd dumped everything that might wash overboard or blow away before the storm, he'd come across her light meter.

Funny thing, the way a woman could burrow under a man's skin. It wasn't like he loved her or anything like that. Oh, hell, no! He was too old to play that game again. Still, he couldn't deny he was looking forward to seeing her.

And he was going to see her, too, if he had to track her all the way to Virginia. Church Grove couldn't be all that big a town. He'd traveled all over the world, and he'd never even heard of Church Grove, Virginia.

A thought occurred to him. What if she was pregnant?

He swore some more and mentally started rearranging the bedroom allocation on the second floor of his new-old house.

Between the morning feeding and opening the daycare center, Deke started her days before the sun was even over the horizon. At four in the afternoon she left the children who hadn't already been picked up with Daisy and Miss Hazel, hurried to Biddy's for another feeding and by the time she had cleaned up after that, she was almost too tired to go apartment hunting.

Her writing was going nowhere. She had toyed briefly with an idea about a boy named Frog who lived on a boat. It had lacked spark. So she'd tried out another idea, this time about a girl who rescued a talking frog and a one-eyed sea captain from a series of disasters, starting with a hurricane. It had had plenty of spark, but she couldn't come up with an ending.

The trouble was, she was hung up somewhere on the other side of reality. The reality of trying to sell an idea in an extremely crowded field. The reality of making a living with no particular marketable skills in a town with no industry. The reality of trying to convince herself that she was on the verge of forgetting Kurt Stryker.

Any day now, Deke told herself, she'd be able to go for hours without thinking a single time of the way he had looked standing up there on the flying bridge, with the wind stirring his thick, sun-streaked hair and blowing his thin khakis against his powerful body. Of the way the muscles in his legs flexed with the roll of the boat.

Of the way he looked when he was amused and trying not to show it. When he was worried and trying not to show it.

Or when he was hurting and trying not to show it.

Darn it, she hadn't asked him to do all the driving! She hadn't asked him to climb all over the *R&R,* tying things down, covering things up, straining wounds that, from the look of the scars, might never fully recover.

She certainly hadn't asked him to make love to her, which must have been excruciating under the circumstances.

She was still pounding her head against an all-too-familiar stone wall when the phone rang. Her heart went into double time, and she nearly tripped on her discarded shoes. It was—

It had to be! She'd known in her deepest heart that it couldn't just end that way.

It wasn't. It was Ambrose Anderson, a nice man she had dated a few times, wanting to know if she would like to drive to Norfolk for dinner tomorrow night.

Ambrose was a pharmacist. He worked in Church Grove's one and only drugstore and was a terrible gossip. If you had a rash, the whole town would know where and how bad. If you had trouble sleeping, if your sinuses were clogged, if you needed a laxative, trust Ambrose to recommend a cure and then tell the whole town about it. There wasn't a malicious bone in his body, he simply liked to talk, and as he had no interests outside his work, he talked about that.

"Ambrose, it sounds wonderful, but between trying to do two jobs and finding someplace to live, I'm bushed." She waited to see if he knew of any possibilities. A couple of rooms in a private home. Even one room—she was that desperate. "Honestly, by the time I get home in the evening, I don't have the energy to move. It's all I can do to nuke my dinner and crawl into bed."

Ambrose recommended a herbal remedy that was guaranteed to restore her energy, put fresh sparkle in her eyes and make her hair grow faster.

She had to laugh. "If it will turn me into a blonde or a redhead, preferably one with natural curls, then I'll take a truckload."

So he told her about his store's line of rinses and home permanents, and she laughed and told him she'd be in in a day or so for her multivitamins, and thanks for the dinner invitation, but no thanks, and then she hung up.

And sighed. If she'd had to go and fall in love again, why couldn't it have been with a nice, safe man like Ambrose? Why did she have to throw her heart away on someone like Kurt Stryker? A man who was technically homeless and who had no interest in settling down again—he'd more or less admitted as much.

On the other hand, he had made room in his life for a boy.

A boy who was going to grow up and leave him in a few years. And then he'd be all alone again, only he would never admit to being lonely.

But he was. Deep down inside, she was convinced that Kurt was every bit as lonely as she was. Deke knew loneliness. She had grown up the center of a loving family, despite the fact that she had lost both her parents at an early age.

She'd still had Granna and her great-aunts. Later on, she'd had Mark. For a little while, at least.

But then, in less than two years, she had lost everyone in her life and had discovered that she was totally without defenses. No antibodies. No immunity from the kind of quiet, desperate loneliness that could stalk a body and hit hurting hard when least expected.

The children at the center had been a godsend. Still were, but it was a shaky operation. She had a feeling it would be closed down before much longer. Not that the care wasn't great, but the facilities fell woefully short of standards.

Even the birds helped a little, but with so many volunteers wandering in and out, some coming from as far away as Norfolk, Biddy didn't really need her.

Kurt did. He needed her. He just didn't know it. He needed her even more than she needed him, because for all their physical strength, men were the weaker sex. They lacked a woman's natural resilience, else why did women statistically outlive men? Why did married men statistically live longer than single ones?

Still lying flat on her yard-sale sofa, Deke pondered statistics. And then she pondered the few days that had changed her life. And then she made up her mind that someone was going to have to rescue Captain Stryker.

So... as long as she had to move anyway, why not look for a place near the water? A place with room for three people and a good school nearby. And a fast-food place and a supermarket.

The trick was going to be persuading Kurt to move to Virginia. To throw in his lot with a pea-poor widow whose earning skills weren't all that great but who was willing to work long and hard to make a home.

Horsefeathers! Maybe she'd better stop trying to write children's books and try her hand at romance. Feisty heroine tackles life head-on, overcomes world-class obstacles to win worthy hero.

And foul-mouthed, ill-mannered, adolescent boy.

Oh, yes, indeedy, she was a master of fiction, all right.

Nine

Kurt found the place finally. It was actually on the map. But if there were any street addresses, they were a well-kept secret. He drove slowly through the center of what could scarcely be called a town and then tackled the side roads. He read names on mailboxes, then remembered that she lived in an apartment. So he drove around some more, looking for something that resembled a multiple-family dwelling.

He'd tried to call her, first from the marina and then from half a dozen stops along the way. There'd been no answer, not even a recorded message on an answering machine. At that point he almost would've settled for that—just hearing the sound of her voice.

The next time he stopped he put in a call to the marina and asked Etheleen if Frog was anywhere around. The kid might've remembered something Kurt had forgotten.

Although there was damned little he'd forgotten about her. In fact, the more frustrated he was in his search, the more he remembered every single detail of the way she looked. She was the only woman he'd ever met who could look desirable when she was sick as a dog from champagne and a choppy sea.

And the way she laughed. And her scent—that sweet, clean, feminine scent that was unforgettable without being at all overwhelming. The way she had of using her hands when she got excited, as if they were small batons orchestrating her thoughts. He thought about the way she had taken to Frog, treating him as an individual and not just a generic kid, even when he was acting up.

Dammit, he *had* to find her. This was getting ridiculous!

Frog had come on the line while Kurt was still recounting all the reasons he was somewhere near the Virginia line in a gas station that advertised beer, collards, red worms and Wolverine shoes instead of in Swan Inlet minding his own business.

"'Sa matter, change yer mind?"

"No, I haven't changed my mind. Look, Frog, do you happen to remember anything Deke said about this place where she lives? Like what it looked like or whether it was in town or out in the country?"

"Lost, huh? I toldja ya shoulda took yer compass. I toldja ya shoulda never gone after 'er," the boy declared.

"Right. And I should've known better than to ask you for help." They'd gone a few rounds when Kurt had first announced his intention of taking a couple of days off in the middle of the week between charters to drive to Virginia. Frog had fired up like a three-year-old being told he had to share his favorite toy.

It hadn't done much to improve matters when Kurt had heard himself sounding just like his own father.

"Kurt, have you split all that kindling yet?"

"Not yet, Pa."

"I should've known better than to ask. Great big football hero like you, you got better things to do than split your mama's kindlin' wood."

Pa hadn't really meant anything by it, but Kurt had had a bad case of thin skin back then. Partly because his words didn't always come out right, but mostly on account of hanging out with guys who didn't know what it was like to have to do the milking, feed up, split kindling and crack the ice on the chickens' water before they caught the bus to school.

With the first money he'd ever earned, he had bought his mama a secondhand electric range. His father had blustered, claimed Kurt was only trying to keep from splitting kindling every morning before he went to school—accused him of being too proud to live in a house where the cooking and the heating were still done with wood.

But his pa had been sort of proud, too. At least, Kurt thought he was. Years later he'd discovered the old man had followed every game he'd ever played, both in high school and at State, and what's more, he had the clippings to prove it.

He thought again of the ballerina music box on his mama's dressing table. The first time he'd ever laid eyes on Deke, she had reminded him of that tiny pirouetting figure. More doll than real woman, he remembered thinking at the time.

Man, had he evermore been wrong.

About four in the afternoon, Kurt ran flat out of patience. Having chased down every cow path and dead-end street in the county, he gave up and pulled in at a place called Anderson's Convenience and Pharmacy.

There were two old women thumbing greeting cards just inside the door and a balding gentleman in a white coat behind the counter. Kurt approached the man. "Would you happen to know where I could find a Ms. Kiley around here? I can't seem to locate the right address." For Deke's sake, he almost hoped the guy wouldn't tell him. It wasn't safe, giving out information to strangers.

Hell, it wasn't even safe asking questions!

"That would be Debranne Kiley. She's the only Kiley around these parts, at least since her husband died. They used to live in that fancy new section, place called Willow Hill, but he died and the house got sold out from under her."

"So where did she go? Where does she live now?"

One of the two women wandered over, a greeting card in hand. "Did I hear you asking about Debranne Kingsly? She was a Kingsly before she married that developer from over to Norfolk, you know. Kingslys lived in these parts since the second supply ship to Jamestown. My third cousin on Mother's side married a—"

"Thanks, ma'am. She's the one I'm looking for, all right. You happen to know where I can find her this time of day? She doesn't answer her phone, and I was sort of worried."

"Oh, no need to worry about Debranne," put in the pharmacist. "She'll be finishing up over at Biddy's most any time now. Once she leaves there, she'll

stop by the post office to pick up her mail, might even
stop in here. She does her grocery shopping on
Thursdays, isn't that right, Miss Cammy?''

Kurt wasn't interested in when she did her grocery
shopping, he wanted to know where he could lay
hands on her right now. ''Yeah, well—I don't have
much of a sense of direction, and Church Grove's not
real good about maintaining street signs, so...''

''Lawsy, who needs street signs? Everybody knows
where everybody lives. Debranne lives in that new
apartment place out on Chesapeake, over by the
cemetery.''

The second woman joined them, a can of antifun-
gus powder and a bottle of Tabu toilet water in her
hand. ''New? Camilla Stevens, that place was built
the year Maude Hobbs married Old Man Adams.
You wore your red coat to the wedding, remember?
And I told you, I said, Cammy, you look just like one
of those—''

A wattled chin wobbled indignantly. ''I remember
what you said. I'm not likely to forget it.''

''Well, it was the truth! That was the same year
Lula Stamp's youngest was killed in that war over in
Korea. You remember, I told you at the time—''

''Can't thank you ladies enough,'' Kurt said dryly.
Now all he had to do was find a blasted cemetery.

Oh, God, he's here, Deke thought as soon as Ambrose told her about the stranger who'd been asking
about her. It was Kurt. It had to be Kurt. Ever since
she'd got the wild idea of finding herself a place by
the water and inviting Kurt and Frog to move in with
her, she'd been quivering in her boots, afraid of actually bursting out in a fit of assertiveness and doing

something embarrassing. Like calling him and asking him what he thought about moving to Virginia.

Or what he thought of meeting her halfway between Swan Inlet and Church Grove for a night of wild, passionate sex.

But what was he doing here? He couldn't be just passing through town on his way to somewhere else, because Church Grove wasn't on the way to anywhere, at least until the new highway got finished.

What if he was waiting for her when she got home? She had finally learned not to wear her good clothes to work, but today she looked like something left over from a flea market. It had been one of those days. One child had vomited on her, one had tested his crayons on the tail of her skirt while she'd been busy mopping up and another one had spilled chocolate milk on her shoes. Add to that the fact that her favorite African Gray had let her have it, right on the shoulder of her yellow blouse, and it truly had not been one of her better days.

"Are you sure it wasn't the UPS man?" she pleaded with the pharmacist. "I ordered some computer paper last week." Oh, goodness, she would die if it was Kurt!

She would die if it *wasn't*.

Deke had stopped by the pharmacy for vitamins and aspirin. Ambrose had come around the counter to greet her, obviously bursting with curiosity. "I know every UPS man who delivers within a hundred miles of Church Grove," he said smugly. "Besides, this fellow wasn't wearing a uniform. He had on a pair of khaki pants and a leather jacket—sort of streaky blond hair—and he was wearing a black patch over one eye. If you ask me, he looked dangerous. I wasn't going to tell him anything, but Miss Camilla and Miss Ada were in here—Miss Ada's still got that fungus under her toenail—and you know how they are. Talk, talk, talk. Debranne?'' he called after her.

But she was gone. Smoothing her hair with one hand, brushing the wrinkles from her stained skirt with the other, Deke hurried out to her car, ground the starter until the engine caught, then headed south on Chesapeake Street. She was half afraid Kurt would find her before she could shower and change into something sexy and wildly flattering and equally afraid he might have grown tired of waiting and left town.

Streaky blond hair and an eye patch. Obviously a dangerous character. Ambrose couldn't possibly know just *how* dangerous.

She parked, grabbed her purse and hastily scanned the half-empty parking lot before reminding herself that she didn't even know what kind of a car he drove.

"Poise and decorum," she muttered to herself, doing the best she could with her flyaway hair with fingers and no mirror. She'd been drilled on poise and decorum before she could even pronounce the words. For years she had thought her grandmother was saying *poison decorum*. A lady, according to Anne Kingsly, remained poised, gracious and unfailingly polite no matter how difficult the situation, because good breeding always won out over boorishness.

But then, Granna Anne had lived in a different world. Ladyhood didn't cut it these days. Not when all the lady in question could think about was how it had felt to lie in her lover's arms. How it felt to stand beside a sparkling harbor under a late afternoon sun and allow herself to be kissed silly by a man with the looks of a handsome pirate and the touch of a gentle prince.

She hadn't dared say a word of what she was feeling at the time, because anything she might have said could and probably would be used against her.

Oh, Lord, he was here!

The lobby looked even more depressing than usual as she shunned the cranky elevator and took the stairs two at a time. Aerobic or not, it was her one concession to fitness training. All she had time for, actually.

And then there he was. Arms draped over his bent knees, he was sitting on the floor, leaning up against her door, looking tired and beautiful and even thinner than she remembered him.

"Kurt?" she whispered tentatively.

"Yeah, what!" Kurt came awake instantly. Years of training. He'd only been dozing, anyway. Not until he'd tracked her to her den had he dared let down his guard, and by then it was too late. Too many days of trying to maintain the boat, run charters, dodge a persistent child welfare worker and oversee the work being done on the house finally caught up with him.

"Sorry," he said, struggling to his feet. "Didn't get much sleep last night." Or the night before, or the night before that. You'd think a man of his age and experience would know better than to waste so much time dreaming about a woman. "Hey, I was in the neighborhood and thought I'd drop by to say hello."

Judas priest, even Frog could do better than that!

"Come inside, I'll make us some coffee. You look as if you could use some. Are you hungry? I've got bacon and eggs and I can stir up a batch of pancakes. I often have breakfast for supper—usually I don't have time to eat breakfast, so I..."

Chatter, chatter, chatter. Lord, woman, you're worse than a cage full of finches!

Kurt followed her inside, yawning, begging her pardon and taking stock of her living quarters all at the same time.

"What in God's name is that thing?" he asked, halting to stare at a piece of furniture that was fully six feet tall, decorated with mirrors, curlicues and half a dozen small balconies, each one sporting at least one framed photograph.

"What? Oh. That's my organ. I told you about it, didn't I? It belonged to my grandmother, and she left it to me when she died. It has real ivory keys, which I think are probably against the law now, but the elephant's already dead, so I don't know what I'm supposed to do about it, because—"

Kurt caught her to him and said, "Hush up, honey, you're babbling." And then he kissed her. Right there between her organ, her computer and her yard-sale sofa, where she had spent countless hours daydreaming about him, he kissed her until she went limp in his arms.

She reached up and captured his ears with her hands, because she needed something to hang on to, and when his tongue caressed hers, and when one of his hands moved up to cover her breast, just below the greenish stain on her shirt, she moaned and sagged all over again.

"I think we'd better sit down," Kurt said hoarsely against the left side of her throat. A flock of goose bumps immediately sprouted along her left flank.

"What about supper?" she asked, more than a hint of desperation in her voice. She was doing it again. Allowing herself to be swept along by the tide. If ever she stood a chance of asserting herself, she was going to have to stop hanging all over him. Men like Kurt Stryker weren't designed to support clinging vines.

Reluctantly, she backed away. "If you'd like to wash up first, it's right through there," she said, trying to remember whether she'd left anything embarrassingly personal lying around.

He got that warm, crinkly look that always made her want to curl up in his lap and hibernate. "I'm okay, but if you want to change into something more comfortable before we talk, feel free."

Talk? Who needed to talk? She could talk when she was by herself—and frequently did. What she wanted to do now involved two people, one bed, and a night that went on forever.

Brilliant. When it comes to learning life's important lessons, woman, you're a dropout.

Deke left him examining her monstrous parlor organ. In her wildest dreams—and she'd had plenty of those—she had never quite been able to picture him in her cluttered living room. In her bed, yes, because a bed was a bed was a bed. Even in her bathtub, because she had a newly discovered kinky turn of mind.

She thought about the small organ stool, and then she thought about those narrow, lumpy bunks aboard the *R&R,* and then she twisted the faucets and waited for the squeaking, gurgling, rumbling to stop and the water to start.

It was just her luck to have him show up on a day when she'd been dowsed in chocolate milk, thrown up upon, scribbled upon, doodooed upon.

Did-did upon?

Whatever.

With a dreamy look on her face, Deke took off her clothes, waited five minutes or so for the water to make its way from the basement up to her antiquated bathroom. The smile—actually, it was more of a smirk—never once left her face.

Kurt took the liberty of washing up in her kitchen sink. Surprisingly, now that he'd seen her he no longer felt tired. He felt energized. And hungry. Not to mention randy as a bull in a pasture full of heifers.

He was staring out the window at the top of a mulberry tree when he heard the bathroom door open and close. He went on staring, bracing himself to act sensibly and say what needed saying before things got too far out of hand.

He had a feeling they were headed that way.

When Deke came out of the bathroom she was wearing what looked like some sort of flowered tent. Her smile was the kind that could melt a glacier. "Hi," she said softly. "Sorry to be so long. It takes a while for the hot water to make it all the way to the second floor. Sometimes it doesn't. In my next apartment, I'm going to try the hot water before I ever sign anything. Fried or scrambled? I can boil them, too, but I never get the timing quite right."

Kurt tried not to stare at her as hungrily as Frog stared at the girl in the tight jeans and the pink Jeep. "Fried. Scrambled. However you want 'em, as long as they're not powdered."

"Scrambled, then. Um . . . crisp or soggy?"

"Are we talking bacon or toast? Because I'm not particular about that, either. Deke. . . .come here, will you? There's something that needs doing, and I don't think it can wait much longer."

Deke didn't even ask what it was, which was a sign of something or other, only she wasn't sure just what. Certainly not poison decorum. With a feeling of inevitability, she crossed the room, her eyes never leaving his face. It seemed to take forever, but it was only a few steps.

Kurt stood and waited, and when she came close enough, he placed both hands on her shoulders and sighed. "I've gone over and over this in my mind, and there's just no easy way to say it."

"To say what?" she breathed. He was leaving the country. He was married and had a slew of children. He had some terrible, terminal disease.

"Look, we both know I'm not a romantic type of guy."

He was a romantic type of guy. He might not think so, but he was. Standing in the doorway, gazing at his back as he stared out her window, she had admired the tilt of his head, the width of his shoulders and his long, lean flanks. Even on dry land, he had the look of a man who'd spent a lot of time on a rolling deck.

He was wildly romantic, and she could only wonder what on earth he saw in her, if he saw anything at all.

She continued to stare at him, forgetting what she'd been about to say. Forgetting to breathe. For all she knew, her heart had forgotten to beat.

"I mean, jeeze—I'll be forty in a couple of years. I just blew practically my whole savings account on a—"

"Kurt."

"I've got a kid I'm hoping to hang on to—at least, I don't own him, but I'd like to keep him around for a while."

"Kurt?"

"And I—yeah, what?"

"Hush," she whispered. He was so close she could see her own reflection in his eye. Without even thinking, she reached up and slid the patch higher on his brow.

Kurt caught his breath. "Ah, God, don't—"

"Let me. I don't want any part of you hidden away. You're so beautiful...even this." Lightly, she touched the flat eyelid that covered the empty socket. There was nothing ugly about it. There could never be anything ugly about him, because whatever he was, he was Kurt. She had seen the scar on his thigh, and hurt because it had hurt him, but she hadn't considered it ugly. It was a part of him, and that was that.

Kurt tilted his head and stared at her water-stained ceiling. And then he lowered his face until his mouth hovered over hers and said, "I want to make love to you, Deke. I don't think I can wait much longer. I did a lot of thinking these past few weeks, but now it's all screwed up in my mind again, and all I can think about is getting you out of that tent and making love to you until I run flat out of steam. Then maybe I can get my head to working again."

He was holding her so close she could feel every muscle, bone and sinew in his body. She could even feel his belt buckle and the buttons on his shirt, which was a pretty good indication of just how sensitive she was to everything about him. "So who's arguing?"

All the air in the room suddenly disappeared. She felt his body stiffen, heard him catch his breath, and then he was rocking her against him until she thought she might go up in flames.

Instead, she stood on tiptoe until her lips brushed his. And then she gave herself up to the sweet, intoxicating spell of desire. Fierce, urgent, honey-sweet desire. It had been weeks since she had felt anything like this.

The first time they had made love, it had been a journey of discovery. Nothing in her brief marriage had prepared her for the way Kurt had made her feel. The second time had been even more special, but in a different way. Before that night in a motel somewhere in a town whose name she couldn't remember, she hadn't known such ecstasy existed.

Now she did. And she felt an irresistible urge to throw caution to the winds and follow her instincts wherever they led, knowing even as she did that she was burning her bridges behind her.

"Give me your lips, Debranne," Kurt whispered, and without waiting, he took them.

They made it to her bed, just barely. Eagerly Deke shed her muumuu while Kurt struggled to free himself of his clothing.

And this time he had protection. Because he had dared hope, not because he had expected. He lowered her onto the bed and came down beside her, acutely aware of the currents and crosscurrents that swirled around them. Aware of the dangers. Aware that not all the dangers were marked on any chart.

"If I start talking too much, will you kindly hush me up?" she pleaded, and he chuckled, but it was a rusty sound.

"That I can promise you, darling." Lying on his side, Kurt gazed at her slight body, at the surprisingly lush curves where her hips flared from a tiny waist. At the delicate, pink-crowned breasts that invited his touch, invited his lips.

Fleetingly, he pictured her belly swollen with his child and knew a moment of disappointment that he hadn't made her pregnant.

He took one earlobe between his teeth and suckled. His mouth moved down her throat, and his hand moved south and homed in on its target. When he felt her stiffen, heard the soft intake of her breath, he nearly went over the edge.

"Come to me, sweetheart," he whispered.

He'd promised himself that this time—if there was a this time—he would take it slow and easy. Using sex as bait to get what he wanted wasn't fair, and he was determined to be fair. But it wasn't easy. Not when sex was all he could think of. When had he built up this conditioned reflex? One look, one touch, and he was hard as a crankshaft.

A man his age—you'd think he would have built up a little natural resistance.

She was toying with the hair on his chest. He thought fleetingly that they really should have talked first, because whatever the outcome, he didn't want any misunderstandings between them.

But then, there was that conditioned reflex. He hadn't counted on that. Should have, but hadn't.

She was breathing shallowly, her lips parted. Her eyes were closed, and it occurred to him that his patch was somewhere in the other room. He hadn't even noticed when he'd lost it.

His fingers brushed through the small dense thicket of golden brown curls. She was hot and damp, and the sweet spicy scent of her desire cut though the last thread of resistance.

Shaking all over, he reached behind him and managed to pull his wallet from his pants pocket. "Wait a minute," he gasped when he felt her small hand surround his throbbing shaft. "Sweetheart, just let me—"

His hands were unsteady. He fumbled and swore and then fumbled again.

"Let me help you," she offered, and then nearly succeeded in driving him out of his mind when her fingers joined his in the task.

By the time he mounted her, trembling with urgency, he was beyond rational thought, beyond all but the desperate drive to assuage the fierce hunger that drove him.

The same hunger—*admit it, Stryker!*—that had driven him all the way to this little nowhere place to find her.

He felt her slender thighs wrap around his waist, felt her hands slide over his sweat-damp back, urging him on and on and on. Taking care to spare her his weight—which meant he would probably suffer for it later, but that was the least of his worries—he began to move. Slowly, slowly at first, because she was small and delicately made, and because he would die rather than hurt her.

And then faster as the exquisite tension rose to un-
bearable heights.

When the moment came, she didn't shout his
name. But the softly voiced, "Yes. Oh, yes..." cut
clean through him to a place he hadn't known existed.

Kurt closed his eye. He had a feeling it was already
far too late for talking.

Ten

___

Outside, through the thin walls, Kurt could hear the sounds of late afternoon traffic. Rush hour in Church Grove, Virginia. Two cars...and then another one. A truck with a gutted muffler, and after a while, another car. A dog barked, and then damned if he didn't hear a cow. It had been years since he'd heard a cow.

He stared at a row of what looked like framed illustrations from a children's book on one wall, and it occurred to him that they probably *were* illustrations from a children's book.

She was a writer, after all.

With her hot little bottom shoved up against his side, Deke slept on. She'd been sleeping for nearly forty-five minutes. Kurt sighed heavily, glanced at a grouping of framed photographs on the other wall and wondered if putting the cart before the horse was considered an art.

If so, he was getting to be a world-class artist.

"Deke," he murmured. "Honey, we need to talk."

"Uh-huh." She made a puffy little sound with her lips, and he refrained from leaning over and kissing her...just barely.

"This would be a lot simpler," he told the sleeping woman beside him, "if I could just file a personnel requisition. Fill in the blanks, detail the specs and whammo. One wife transferred to Stryker headquarters."

Kurt had a feeling he might be getting in over his head.

He also had a feeling it was far too late to do much about it.

Reluctantly, he sat up, swung his legs off the bed and stood. Considering the way he felt, he might have just crawled out of a sauna after a three-day sweat. Beside him, Deke stirred in her sleep, and he thought maybe he'd better grab a cold shower before he tried to make his case. He had a feeling that if he hung around here much longer, he might complicate matters by making love to her all over again. She had that effect on him.

Ten-*shun!*

By the time Kurt emerged from the bathroom, his wet hair several shades darker, his good eye several degrees brighter, Deke was awake and stirring. She had secured herself behind the same flowery tent she'd worn earlier. It covered her from chin to toes and all the way out to her fingertips. If she thought that old business about out of sight, out of mind was going to help her, she was way off course. Maybe a chastity belt and a flak jacket...

It still wouldn't be enough.

"So... you're awake. I was going to surprise you and fix us something to eat." He shouldn't have slept with her. Not this time, at least. At least not until he'd laid out the ground rules. This wasn't your standard hearts-and-flowers romance, but the way he'd been going at it, he could see how she might misunderstand.

Deke glanced at the clock on the bedside table. Nine-oh-seven. She stared at the white crocheted rug. She frowned at her thumbnail, nibbled it, and finally, she looked at him. "Yes, well...I can do that."

"Deke, I want you to know—"

Her smile was as fragile as one of those crystal champagne glasses she'd taken aboard the boat. "You don't need to say anything, Kurt. We're both adults."

"Meaning?"

"Meaning, um—the way we affect each other. It— well, it just sort of took me by surprise right at first, because..."

"Because?" Kurt leaned against the doorframe. He was beginning to enjoy her performance. And he'd thought *he* was having trouble dealing with whatever this thing was that had sprung up between them. Hell, compared to her, he was an ace.

"It's only chemical," she said earnestly.

"Sure. I knew that."

"According to this article I read, it's called phero-mones—it's got something to do with moths, but evidently people are affected, too. This invisible chemical that makes people feel—I mean, it makes them want to—well, anyway, when certain people get close to certain other people, it produces this invisible gas or something, called pheromones, and they have to be careful, or. . ."

"Or?" Kurt prompted. She was all revved up and ready to rattle, as if talking fast would solve everything. He'd noticed that about her before—that she chattered when she was feeling off-balance. It made him want to hold her, soothe her, comfort her. Which would inevitably start the whole cycle all over again.

"Look, why don't I make us some coffee and we'll talk things over, nice and calm and sensible. If you're afraid of this pherowhatsis, I'll stay on my side of the room and you can stay on yours."

"It's not all that big," Deke said dolefully. "My living room, I mean. And I'm hungry for more than just coffee."

Yeah, so was he.

The phone rang, and she hurried to answer it. "Saved by the bell," Kurt jeered softly.

A few minutes later she replaced the receiver, took a deep, bracing breath and said, "It was only Ambrose, wanting to know if I was all right."

"Are you?"

"Well, of course I am. I'm just fine. Kurt, don't take this personally, but sleeping together isn't all that big a deal these days. I mean, people do. All the time. Even on TV."

"On TV, too, huh? Is that with or without the rabbit ears?"

Her lips quivered. Her eyes sparkled. Having an irreverent sense of humor herself, she appreciated it in others. "You know what I mean. As long as we're careful not to—that is, as long as we don't—well, you know what I mean,'' she said, wondering how he could possibly know when she didn't know herself.

Kurt knew exactly what she meant. It was one of the reasons he was having such a hard time concentrating. Leaning against the doorframe, he wondered how long it would be before she tripped over her tongue. Her face was pink and earnest and she was picking at a thread that might easily bring about the downfall of that whatchamacallit she was wearing.

And he was losing sight of his mission again.

Get it in gear, Stryker. He cleared his throat. "You asked if I was just passing through town. Well, the truth is, I came here looking for you. You remember I mentioned this social worker who's been giving me a hard time about—"

Relief flooded her face as the phone shrilled again. Impatiently, Kurt tapped his foot and tried to remember where he'd left off. The social worker. Home—traditional family unit—wife. Silently, he went over his carefully planned speech while Deke assured Miss Cammie that yes, her young man had found her, but he wasn't really her young man, he was only a friend who was passing through town.

"Passing through town?" he repeated softly.

She glared at him. "I had to say something," she whispered, covering the receiver with the palm of her hand. She reassured Miss Cammie that she was just fine, she really was, and that he wasn't really a dangerous man, he only looked that way.

"I do?" Kurt teased after she hung up.

"Actually, that was one of the first things I noticed about you. That you looked dangerous. Sort of like the pirate in *Peter Pan* in this amateur production I saw once in Richmond.''

Kurt held up one hand. "Look, Ma, no hook," he said, grinning.

"Yes, well . . . you have to understand how it is in small towns. Swan Inlet is a bustling resort compared to Church Grove.''

She smiled, Kurt chuckled, and then they were both laughing. "Now, what was it you were saying about a social worker? Does it have anything to do with Frog?''

Leaving the support of the doorframe, Kurt steered her toward the kitchen, which was about the size of a walk-in closet. While she set about frying bacon and beating eggs for a late supper, he leaned his hips against a counter, crossed his arms over his chest and launched into his proposition.

Or proposal.

Whatever.

"You're going to have to move in a few weeks anyway, right?" he said by way of a romantic prologue.

"As soon as I can find a place," she corrected, grating cheese into the eggs. "Most of the tenants are already gone.''

"What would you think about relocating?''

She cut him a suspicious glance. "I've considered it. Why do you ask?''

Good sign, Kurt told himself. She'd considered it. Which meant it wasn't entirely out of the question. "Why don't we move on to the next line? Did you ever consider remarrying?''

The cheese grater struck the floor with a clatter. Kurt leaned over to pick it up, Deke leaned over to pick it up, and heads bumped. Kurt caught her by the shoulders and dragged her against him. With a soft oath he gave up all pretense at subtlety. "Deke, will you please marry me?"

She looked cute and sexy as all get-out, even with her mouth hanging open. "What did you just say?" she whispered.

"I believe I just asked you to marry me. I was trying to lead up to it gradually, sort of work it into the conversation, but I'm not real good at this sort of thing."

Deke's ears were ringing. She suspected it might have something to do with her accelerated heart rate. "But—why?"

"Why not?"

Which was not precisely the response she'd been hoping for. "Well, for one thing, we haven't known each other very long."

"How long did you know What's His Name?"

"Mark? A few weeks. And look how that turned out."

"Well, if it's any comfort to you, I don't fly any more. Depth perception's shot all to hell with the eye thing."

Deke murmured, "Oh, heavens," and plopped down into one of the three dinette chairs. Kurt rescued the burning bacon.

"Look, don't get me wrong. I don't expect any great story-book romance or anything like that, but if you look at it from a rational point of view, it makes sense. We're both single and unattached. I'm self-employed. Doing pretty well, with prospects to do even better. You've got a portable job—at least, your writing's portable. I don't know how hooked you are on your other jobs, but if you gave them up you'd have more time for writing. And since you're going to be moving anyway..."

He broke off, thinking there had to be a simpler way to go about this business of getting himself a wife. He didn't recall getting all tongue-tied with Evelyn.

Actually, Evelyn had been the one to pop the question, although they'd both pretended afterward that he had. But then she'd gone down to Seattle to shop for her trousseau, and he'd gone down off Montague Island in high winds and rough seas. Saved the boy, his old man and the dog, and in the process busted up his body pretty bad. After that, his big romance had gone south, only Evelyn hadn't wanted to talk about it. She'd never been real good at facing reality.

Which was the main reason that this time he wanted everything out in the open, right up front. No unpleasant surprises. No hanging around the church trying to look like he didn't give a hoot that his fiancée had gotten cold feet and skipped out on him. Socially, it was embarrassing as hell.

Kurt waited for her to speak. Deke waited for him to continue. Quickly, he went over what he'd just said to see if he'd left anything out, or worse yet, said anything he shouldn't have said. He figured she was too sensible to expect one of those hand-over-heart, knee-to-the-floor jobs. On the other hand, all he knew about women was that he didn't know much about women.

Kids, now, that was a different matter. He got along just great with Frog. Rescue victims? He'd dealt with all kinds, all ages and all sexes over the years. Some of them worked through shock by talking a mile a minute. Some of them didn't talk at all. Some just needed a warm body to hang on to until they quit shaking and realized they were still alive.

"Is that it? Some social worker is breathing down your neck and you need a wife to convince her to let you adopt Frog?"

Kurt let out his breath in one long, relieved gust. "That's the gist of it, but adoption's out. Frog's probably still got a mother somewhere. The trouble is, nobody's heard from her in a few years, and the kid needs somebody now."

"Does Frog want me?"

"Well, now, as to that..." He raked his fingers over the back of his head and realized he wasn't wearing his patch. It was the first time he'd ever gone without it in mixed company. "Look, I won't kid you. Right now he's sore as hell because he thinks I like you better than I like him—which is crazy."

He was studying the tip of his shoe, else he might've noticed her stricken expression. "The boy and I, we've been together more than two years now. We've built up a lot of equity in this relationship, and I don't want to see him dragged off to start all over again in a different situation. He's at a vulnerable stage in life. Too old for his age in a lot of ways—still just a kid in other ways. I don't want him farmed out to a bunch of strangers."

But Deke had stopped listening several sentences back. *He thinks I like you better than I like him— which is crazy.*

Well, of course it was crazy, she told herself once she'd swallowed the lump in her throat. Kurt had spent more than two years with Frog. He'd known her only a few weeks. He wouldn't even be here now if he didn't need her help.

Of course, there was still that pheromone business. . . .

"What about someone else? I mean, surely you know other women who would jump at the chance to marry you."

His grin was just as quirky and crinkly as ever, except for a certain bleakness in his eye. "Well...there's Etheleen," he said. "She runs the marina for the guy who owns it. I reckon if I paid her enough, she might consider taking us on. The trouble is, I've never been real partial to women who chew tobacco and wear men's felt hats and roll their nylons down around their ankles."

"Seriously, Kurt, there must be someone."

"Seriously, Deke, there is. Someone whose company I enjoy a whole lot. Someone I respect. A lady who has all the qualities I like most in a friend. Add to that, she's got this sexy way of moving that reminds me of a music box my mama used to have, and—"

"Your mama had a sexy music box?"

"Hush up, woman, I'm on a roll. The thing is, even if it weren't for the boy, I wouldn't mind being married to this woman. In fact, the more I think about it, the better I like the idea."

Deke's eyes were glittering like wet amber. She knocked over a cup, salted the eggs twice and said, "Then there's only one problem as far as I can see. Even if she'll have you, you don't have anywhere to put her, unless she'll agree to sleep on deck, and even—"

The phone startled a yelp out of her. "Honestly! This is the most my phone has rung all month." She dried her hands on her muumuu, brushed past him and hurried into the living room.

Kurt gave a silent cheer. It was working! She knew damned well he was talking about her—who else fit the description? And she was right there with him all the way, hooked, gaffed and all but landed.

"Kurt, it's for you," she called out, peering around her monstrous, multistory organ.

He frowned. No one knew where he was—no one except Etheleen. Which meant that either the boat had sprung a leak or he had messed up his schedule and a charter had turned up—or the IRS had sent a posse after him for mailing in his last quarterly a day late.

Ten minutes later, Deke sent him off with a bacon and egg sandwich and a mug of coffee. She didn't offer to go with him, and Kurt didn't ask her to. Frog was missing. Etheleen hadn't seen him since early that morning when she'd walked down to leave his monthly bill for mooring space and utilities. The boat had been all battened down, the salon hatch locked. Normally, they only locked up when they were both going to be gone for several hours.

The school bus had stopped, honked and then driven off, and Etheleen had worried. She'd called around and discovered that no one had seen the boy since early that morning, which wasn't unusual except that he hadn't gone to school and he hadn't stopped by Joe's to stock up on cheeseburgers. She'd thought Kurt might want to know.

"Let me know as soon as you find him," Deke had said, and Kurt had promised he would. His eye had said a lot more than that, but she didn't dare allow herself to interpret. Didn't dare!

Like a sleepwalker, she went about cleaning up the mess in the kitchen, then remembered that she still hadn't eaten anything. She tried to calculate when he'd be getting to Swan Inlet, but then, she was a cautious driver and she had a feeling Kurt might not be. Not under the circumstances.

Oh, Lord, she loved him so awfully much.

Still in a trance, she made herself a peanut butter and marmalade sandwich and left it on the third balcony of the organ alongside the framed snapshot of her mother in her wedding dress.

She stared out the window, watched the first star come out over Mr. Etheridge's satellite dish and then sank down and had herself a long, noisy cry, after which she felt somewhat comforted. Kurt would find Frog. The boy was young, for all he tried to appear so tough. If someone had come around asking questions, he might have been frightened enough to run, but once Kurt got home, he'd come out of hiding. And Kurt would call and tell her so. And after a while maybe they could pick up more or less where they'd left off.

Or maybe not...

Deke told herself, because there was no one else to tell, that Kurt really did like her. Unless she had misunderstood him, he had asked her to be Frog's mama. More or less. And he wasn't talking about any marriage of convenience, either, because there was that pheromone thing.

So. She just might do it.

She just might marry the man and *make* him fall in love with her! A frog, a prince and a determined princess. What more did a story need for a happy ending?

Eleven

Search and rescue. Even though it was long past midnight and he was short on sleep, Kurt hit the ground running, having already gone over the list of possibilities. Flying air-sea rescue missions was one thing. Finding a street-smart kid who didn't want to be found was something else.

He had a sneaking suspicion Frog wanted to be found, only not until he'd made his point, whatever that was. He was pretty sure it had something to do with Deke, and if that was the case, they were just going to have to work it out because Kurt wasn't about to give up either one of them.

Not that he had them. But dammit, he was going to! One way or another, he was going to rein in the pair of them, because whether or not they were ready to admit it, they needed him.

And, yeah—he needed them.

He got in touch with the sheriff's office.

"You've got the description?" he asked, and was assured that half the law east of the Mississippi had the description. For a two-bit crook, Junior Smith had had a pretty long rap sheet. Frog was no longer a skinny, hungry-looking tagalong child with freckles, big front teeth and even bigger brown eyes.

Instead, he was a skinny, hungry-looking adolescent with freckles, big front teeth and even bigger brown eyes. Eyes that could reach right inside where a man lived and twist the living hell out of his heart.

"Yeah, well...leave a message at the marina if you get any leads," he said gruffly. "I'll check in hourly."

At a time like this he could have used a cellular phone, but in a fringe area like Swan Inlet it wouldn't be too reliable. Etheleen was.

As soon as school opened, he went around to the office. Next he checked in at Joe's Place. He even waylaid the girl in the pink Jeep, who struck him as only marginally brighter than a green-head fly. He was stumped. There weren't that many places a kid could hide in a place the size of Swan Inlet.

Briefly, he considered contacting social services. It was a risk, but they just might know something.

On the other hand, if he knew Frog—and after two years, he was getting to know him pretty well—he'd steer well clear of any authority. They both knew their situation was pretty shaky. The last thing Frog would risk was having a swarm of child welfare workers come down on him to put the screws on his preferred life-style.

By that evening, Kurt was no further ahead than when he'd started searching. The good news was that none of the hospitals within a two-hundred-mile range had reported an accident victim who fit the description.

The bad news was that he had run flat out of places to look. Waiting patiently was not an option. He'd run out of patience about the same time he'd checked the boat and found that Frog had taken his new boots but no schoolbooks. Two CDs, but no player. All the loose change in the box they emptied their pockets in every night, but not a single dollar of the emergency fund in the coffee can in the bait locker.

He had also taken the last of the cinnamon buns, a jar of pickled eggs and a blanket.

So he called Deke. There was nothing she could do, nothing to report, but he'd promised to keep her posted.

Oh, hell, the real reason was that he felt this fierce need to reach out and touch her any old way he could.

It took him a minute to get his brain on line when he heard her voice. He could picture her just as clearly as if he was in the same room with her, and suddenly he wanted her here. Right beside him. He'd wanted her before, which was why he'd gone haring off to Virginia on some crackpot excuse, but this was a different kind of wanting.

However, this wasn't the time to explore those differences. Instead, he told her what he'd done and what he was planning to do next. Which was to talk to Alex, who had a teenage daughter and who might, just might, have some clue as to how the teenage mind worked.

"Yeah, I know—it's a stretch, but I'm running out of ideas."

"Oh, Kurt, I just wish..."

He could picture her gnawing on her lower lip. "What? What do you wish, Debranne?" He couldn't hide his exhaustion, didn't even try to hide the worry in his voice. A damp northeast wind was pressing against his back as he slumped against the semi-enclosed phone booth. Sometime during the past half hour it had started to rain. This had to be the rainiest season in years.

"I just wish I could think of something to help, but I can't. The last time I saw him he seemed to be angry over something—or maybe he was just worried. I thought it might be about school, or something that had happened on the trip, but maybe it was just my imagination."

"It wasn't your imagination," Kurt said, wanting desperately to share his worries but determined not to. A man who couldn't handle his own problems had no business involving a woman. Even a willing one. "Look, I'll handle this. He'll turn up in the morning, wanting breakfast. Tomorrow's Friday. We're booked both Saturday and Sunday, and he's not about to pass up his tips."

Kurt got off the phone and congratulated himself on not whining, not spilling his guts. Not begging her to get herself on down here and help him hold it together.

But God, he needed her with him. Not that she could do anything—he simply needed her beside him.

Deke had heard what Kurt had said as well as what he hadn't said. She had never knowingly relied on instinct—it might've been better if she had—but right now every instinct she possessed was urging her to drop everything and go. Just go.

Never mind waiting for an invitation. Never mind that she'd spent the entire time after Kurt left her working off an excess of nervous energy. She'd felt compelled to accomplish something. Anything! After watching his taillights disappear, she had gone inside and in a mood of sheer recklessness called Biddy's and the day-care center and begged off both her jobs for a few days.

It had helped neither her ego nor her sense of security to be told that she wasn't really needed. "Lawsy, I've got the folks swarming all over the place wanting to play with the birds. You spend some time with your young man, honey, we'll make out just fine."

Her young man? Mercy, did the whole town have extrasensory perception? The mind boggled!

Word from the day-care center was more reassuring. "All those sick stomachs yesterday? It wasn't the pudding like we thought. Half the kids are out again, so you might as well take a little vacation. Daisy and me'll manage just fine," Miss Hazel told her. "You sit down and write yourself another book, y'hear?"

Oh, yes. Just like that. Take a few hours off, whistle up her muse, and the book was as good as written.

She had tried, though. Spent hours at it. Then she'd tossed out everything she had written and started packing. Started and finished, because she really didn't have that much to pack. That done, she called every rental listed in the Norfolk paper that sounded even faintly likely and made arrangements to look at the only two in Church Grove. Actually, one of them wasn't even in Church Grove, it was in Suffolk County.

So now she was bone tired again, her hair was a mess—her whole life was a mess—and she was fixing to drive all night because her highly unreliable instinct kept whispering that Kurt needed her.

What *she* needed was a brain transplant.

It took almost all her available cash to fill the tank of her car, which meant she would have to sleep either in the back seat or aboard the *R&R*. Heaven alone knew what she would live on once the emergency was over, never mind where. At this rate, she wouldn't even be able to pay a security deposit, much less hire a mover.

"Where, where, where?" she mumbled. "If I was a frightened child trying to prove something to somebody, where would I be?"

She had hid in the attic for nearly an hour once after she'd broken a prized antique vase, but she'd come downstairs again when she'd had to go to the bathroom. Even as a rebel, she'd been a failure.

The rain started just south of the Virginia-North Carolina state line. A drizzle, not a downpour. She switched on the windshield wipers and wished she had stopped off for coffee at that last place she'd passed. It was too late now. Everything was closed.

Where, where, where could he have gone?

Kurt would be sick with worry. For all he pretended to have everything under control, she knew better. Under all that sexy man-of-the-sea machismo there was one sweet, sensitive, loving man who was worrying himself sick.

She tried singing to keep up her spirits, but it took too much energy, so she switched on the radio. The news came on. There was nothing about any runaway child, so she switched it off again. Mentally, she ran through her repertoire of quotations that occasionally served to focus her mind or settle her stomach, but none of them fit the occasion.

"'Train up a child in the way he should go, and when he is old, he will not depart from it,'" she quoted, and then, thinking of the little she knew about Frog's earlier life, she whispered, "Oh, no!"

But Frog wasn't old. Besides, he'd had the advantage of living with Kurt for the past couple of years. That ought to count for something.

It was just past midnight when she pulled into the marina. The security light cast a harsh, unreal glow over the deserted parking lot. Kurt's was the only truck there. She peered into the office, through the salt-clouded windows. A light was burning, but there was no one there. She had half expected the place to be crawling with volunteer searchers. Didn't they always do that when a child was missing?

Turning away, she picked out the pale shape of the *R&R* moored in her regular place and saw the faint yellowish glow of a light inside the salon. Without even pausing to think, she snatched up her overnight bag, slammed out of her car and made a dash through the rain, her courage fading with every step she took. Dear God, she had done it again. Acted on sheer impulse without thinking things through.

So now what?

Standing on the freshly repaired wharf, Deke was torn between barging ahead and slinking off into the night. She didn't know the protocol for uninvited guests. Did one ask permission to come aboard? She couldn't even knock on his door without first boarding his boat. Would that make her a trespasser?

She was still wavering, torn between abject cowardice and aggressive empowerment, when the hatch slid open to reveal Kurt silhouetted against the yellow light inside.

"You're here." He didn't even sound surprised.

"Nothing yet?" she asked, dropping her bag into the cockpit. Her awkwardness was gone. This was where she belonged.

He shook his head, stepped forward quickly to swing her aboard, and then they simply held on to each other. Deke knew as well as she knew her own name that she loved this man with every muscle in her body, and if a soul had muscles, then those, as well.

"I had to come," she said simply.

"I knew you would. I'd have asked you, but—"

"I don't know how I can help, but I wanted—"

"Yeah, me, too. I almost asked you, but it didn't seem fair."

"Fair has nothing to do with it."

"To be honest, I thought it might show weakness."

"Weakness?" She leaned back in his arms and stared up at his flawed and beautiful face. He wasn't wearing his patch. His hair looked as though he'd been raking his fingers through it. There were signs of strain around his eyes, his mouth...and she loved him so much she ached with it.

"I've looked everywhere I know to look. Either he hitched a ride and left town or he's somewhere nearby, waiting for..."

"Waiting for what?"

Kurt shook his head. "God knows." He ushered her into the salon, out of the cold, blowing drizzle. There was a pot of hard-boiled coffee bubbling on a gas ring, and Deke poured two mugs and fixed his the way he liked it without thinking. They sat across the table from one another. Now that she was here, it didn't seem quite so necessary to touch him constantly. It felt as if they were touching even when they weren't.

"I keep thinking there's something I've missed. Something obvious," he said.

"That girl—the one he likes? Have you talked to her?"

"Josie? She said he was too uncool for words, but if she noticed him following her or anything, she'd send him on home."

Deke came to a swift boil. "That—that little *twit!*"

A bleak smile flickered across Kurt's face. "Yeah, but as Frog says, she's got a great pair of bazongas."

Glancing at her own modest bazongas, Deke fought down a surge of assertiveness. Anger wasn't going to solve anything. "Where did he like to go? Where's he been spending his free time lately? Does he have any special friends? Have you talked to them?"

"Answer number one, he likes to go fishing when there's a chance of a big tip. Even when there's not. For a kid who'd never been fishing until a couple of years ago, he took to it like a—"

"Like a fish to water," she finished, and they both smiled. "So I guess you've checked out all the other boats."

Kurt nodded. "He's got a couple of boys he hangs with at school. They say he's been real quiet ever since the night of the game."

"Could something have happened on the trip? Besides losing the game, I mean?"

Kurt toyed with his mug, not meeting her eyes. Something had happened, all right. Only he wasn't sure, even now, just how deep it went. He had a feeling there were still a few land mines in the boy's past and evidently knowing that Kurt and Deke had spent a night together had tripped a wire.

Abruptly, he got up and began to pace. Three strides in any one direction brought him to a halt. The small salon teemed with frustrated energy. Deke remained silent. When Kurt quietly slammed a fist into the door of a wooden locker, she rose and went to wrap her arms around him from behind.

At least he didn't shove her away. His hands closed over hers, and he said, "I don't know what else to do. I just don't know. God."

Deke lay her head against his back. "Sleep. You'll need your strength for tomorrow."

"Today." He glanced at a clock mounted on the bulkhead and swore.

"Once it's light enough, we'll cover every road, every path—every possible place."

"I've already done that. He could be miles away."

"He could be close by, too. The only security he has is right here. With you. Why would he throw that away?"

"I don't know. Maybe because he thought I was planning to throw him away. It wouldn't be the first time he'd been treated like a piece of garbage." He swore some more.

"Hush now," she murmured. She wanted to say, yes, she would marry him, because her life was already so inextricably interwoven with his that a mere ceremony seemed superfluous. The fact that she had known him for only a few weeks didn't seem to matter. Evidently, she wasn't as sensible and levelheaded as she'd thought. Not where love was concerned. Maybe no woman was.

But now was not the time. "Kurt, lie down for a little while. Close your eyes. Try to relax, and something will come to you, I know it will. Your unconscious mind knows a lot more than your conscious mind does."

He gave a bitter bark of laughter. "It could hardly know less. Ah, Deke—I'm sorry I got you involved in all this. It's not your problem."

"Of course it's my problem. I care about you and you care about him, so that makes it my problem."

Still holding her, he turned her in his arms and buried his face in her hair. "You make it all sound so simple."

"Lie down. Close your eyes and clear all the clutter from your mind. It *is* simple."

Dear Lord, it had better be, she told herself, because she was walking in no-man's-land. For the first time in her life, she felt like a tower of strength. It didn't make sense, but then, what in her life had ever made sense? If she'd invented her own life as a plot, it would have been rejected as being either too dull or too utterly implausible.

Kurt made a bed on the floor—the deck, he called it—because the sleeping benches were too far apart. They held each other, and there was nothing sexual about it.

Well...almost nothing sexual. It was there, all right—the pheromones—but they were both too tired and too worried to do much about it, so they held each other, taking comfort in the warmth of being in the arms of a loved one, and whether Kurt was ready to admit it or not, Deke knew he loved her.

They might even have slept.

Rain clouds were still blocking the sun, making it seem earlier than it was, when Deke sat up with a start. Kurt was gone. Her bedroom was gone. It took her a moment to bring things into focus, and by that time she heard voices outside.

"You the guy that ordered the load of gravel? Hey, man, I can't deliver it until that place of yours dries up. We got halfway down the road and almost sunk up to the axle."

Which was how they came to be, some twenty minutes or so later, on a narrow dirt road between a scrubby woodland and a muddy wetland, heading for Oyster Point.

"It's a long shot," Kurt said, "but you need to see it since I've fixed it up."

"I do?"

"Yeah, well... remember when I asked you to marry me? I was fixing to tell you about what I'm doing and how I thought you might want to pick out the colors and all."

"I didn't even know the house survived the storm. I thought all you had to live in was your boat."

"It survived. The old place is tough." By that time they were pulling up before the gaunt old house, which was surrounded by scaffolds and piles of sand and gravel. The yard was a soggy, rutted mess, but the view was magnificent.

And there he was.

Kurt was out of the truck in an instant, striding across the littered expanse, his gait more uneven than ever. Deke thought, *A decent bed will help that little matter,* and then she thought, *Oh, thank the Lord Frog's safe,* and then she thought, *I'm going to twist that boy's ear real good for scaring Kurt half to death!*

"You wanna do some explaining?" Kurt asked, his voice rough with anger and relief. Deke hung back, but she could hear him all the same over the sound of wind through the marsh grass and the squawk of feeding gulls.

Frog shrugged his bony shoulders. He had a blanket wrapped around him, but he looked cold and pinched and hungry. But then, he always looked hungry. When he didn't reply, Kurt tried again.

"Next time you want to camp out, leave a note, will you?"

"Hey, man, chill out. What's got you so bent outta shape, anyhow? It's not like I took nothin'!"

And then his eyes found Deke, and he suddenly looked as if he might cry. This time, Deke didn't even try to think things through. She jumped down from the truck, landing in a yellow puddle of mud, and slogged her way across to where the pair of them stood on a bare, unfinished front porch.

"Don't you ever, ever scare us this way again, Frog Smith! Do you know what your father's been through? Do you know what I've been through, picturing all sorts of awful things that could have happened to you?"

"He ain't my father," Frog mumbled.

"No, he's not! What he is is the best friend you ever had, and I think you're too smart to throw that away. So—the question is, why did you do it? Was it because of me? Because you don't like me?"

Both males tried to speak, but she sliced through the air with a small hand, cutting them off. "I don't want to hear it. Now you listen here to me, both of you. If we're going to make this thing work, we've all got to make up our minds to level with each other, right?"

Kurt looked as if he'd gone fishing for pinfish and hooked into a blue marlin. Frog looked... well, mostly he looked hungry.

"Right," she repeated, hands on her hips. Without waiting for a response, she said, "In the first place, I love your—well, whatever he is to you. I love him until I can't even do my work properly for thinking about him, but that's beside the point."

"You do?" Kurt asked wonderingly.

"Hush up, I'm not finished yet. As for you—" She drilled Frog with both barrels. "I'm prepared to be every bit as good a friend to you as Kurt is, and whether or not you know it, you're going to be needing a woman's advice. We women know a lot about—well, about things."

Frog started to grin. "You mean like cooking?"

"No, I don't mean like cooking, I mean about girls. And—well, I can, but I'm not all that good at it."

"About girls?"

"About cooking," she snapped. "The first thing we need to do is get you somewhere warm and feed you. I'll bet you haven't had a bite to eat in days, have you?"

"No, ma'am. Not hardly nothing."

She opened her mouth to remark on the triple negative, but Kurt elbowed her in the side, and she closed her mouth.

"I think we'd better do what the lady says, don't you? We can settle the details later. By the way, you've got some homework to catch up on if you expect to go out with me tomorrow."

A long time later, Kurt joined Deke at Montrose's Motor Inn, where he'd booked her a room as his fiancée. Gossip was already making the rounds. There were times when he wished Swan Inlet wasn't such a small place, but there were other times, such as now, when he didn't give a sweet damn in hell where he was or what was said about it as long as she was there with him.

"Is he all right?" Deke asked anxiously when Kurt closed the door, fixed the safety chain and shed his leather jacket.

"Stuffed to the gills and out like a light. I gave him a pass on homework, but he's going to have to make it up this weekend."

She came into his arms as naturally as a flower turned to the sun. "Nobody ever said it was easy...raising children."

"We've got a lot of lost time to make up for. A lot of bad history to overcome."

He was nuzzling the side of her neck in that place that sent goose bumps coursing down her flank. "He's worth it."

"Damn right he is."

They were down to broken murmurs, neither of them thinking about the long years ahead, both of them thinking of more immediate concerns. Like how quickly they could shed their clothes. How wild and utterly wonderful it was to have found each other against all odds. How long it would take to arrange things so that they could be together for keeps.

A long time later, Kurt lay exhausted on his back with Deke sprawled across his body. He couldn't bear to let her get farther away than that. "Did I tell you I love you?" he murmured.

"You didn't have to. I knew it."

He quirked an eyebrow. His patch was somewhere on the floor, along with his clothes. He was going to have to clean up his act and quit diving into the nearest bed the minute he saw her.

"Pretty sure of yourself, aren't you?"

"No, not really," Deke drawled sleepily. "Only, if there's one thing I do know, it's happy endings. All children's books have them. They're as necessary as—as, well, vitamins."

"I thought you were going to say love."

"That goes without saying."

Kurt sighed with contentment. His body was already reacting to the feel of her small breasts pressing on his chest, of the burning heat pooled in her loins...and in his. "Honey, I've got news for you. It's not going to go without saying in our house. Maybe if I say it often enough, I'll come to believe I finally got lucky."

"There are lots of different ways of saying I love you," she whispered, and proceeded to demonstrate a few.

Epilogue

The sun shone down with fierce splendor over a parking lot filled with pickup trucks, beach buggies, a few cars, one pink Jeep and one John Deere tractor. Errol Flynn Gaskill's car wouldn't start. Most of the wedding guests lined the wharf, as there was room in the cockpit of the *R&R* for only the preacher, the bride and groom, the best man and a very pregnant Mariah Wydowski, wife of one of Kurt's two best friends, who had offered to stand up with Deke in the absence of any other candidates.

Frog, resplendent in his very first suit and tie, which, contrary to expectations, they hadn't had to hog-tie him and force him into, paid more attention to the wedding guests than he did to his duties as best man. To one wedding guest, at least. The girl in the pink Jeep wiggled her fingers at him and giggled.

Alex, Kurt's other best friend, and his new wife, Angel, had taken over preparations for the reception at Oyster Point, while Gus Wydowski dealt with what he termed the organ transplant. He'd sent a truck and crew north to haul Deke's belongings, organ included, to Swan Inlet, where the organ would go even more out of tune on account of the humidity. Not that it mattered. Nobody ever played it, anyway, but having it around was like having a part of her family there.

"Dearly beloved, friends and— My Lord, will someone please turn off that noise?"

Frog ducked inside the salon and shut off the CD player.

"Now, where were we? Dearly beloved, we are gathered here today in the sight of—"

Someone yelled from the parking lot, "Hey, Kurt, the blues have hit the Cape. Big 'uns! Feller caught one that weighed near on to forty-five pounds!"

There was an immediate exodus of trucks, with the John Deere chugging along behind.

A few minutes later, a gray truck with a construction company logo on the door pulled up beside the marina office. Rising several feet above the cab was a monstrous shape covered with canvas and secured with ropes. "Hey, somebody wanna tell me where to put this thing? It weighs a ton and a half!"

"I'll go show 'em!" Frog cried, and Kurt reached out and grabbed him by the necktie.

"Not yet, you won't. We're going to get through this wedding before anyone else moves a foot from this place, is that clear? Now, Reverend Stowe, if you'd be so kind, I'd like to take me a bride, and then we can all head on out to Oyster Point and—"

"Pig out!" shouted Frog.

Kurt turned to the woman at his side. She was wearing a peach-colored suit with a lacy gadget at the throat. Her hair was blowing across her face, her cheeks were pink—so was the tip of her nose—and her eyes were suspiciously bright. She had never looked more beautiful. "Are you sure you know what you're getting into, sweetheart? I think we're about to get to the part about for better or for worse, so if you want out now, you'd better speak up fast."

A big outboard roared past, the crew waving and yelling congratulations. The huge wake rocked every boat in the marina. Deke clutched Kurt's arm and yelled over the noise, "If you think I'm giving up that easy, you don't know your woman. Reverend Stowe? If you please?"

And so they were married. On Thanksgiving day, with friends and acquaintances gathered around—at least those who hadn't gone fishing. Much later that day, half a dozen or so of the guests lingered over the remnants of a barbecue feast. Etheleen wept a little, but mostly she was too busy playing with Alex and Angel's infant son. Frog and Sandy, Alex's teenage daughter, compared shoe sizes. Gus made his pregnant wife lie down on Deke's yard-sale sofa and then sat beside her, feeding her from his own plate. She and Angel had spent the afternoon discussing what kind of shrubs and trees would grow best in the low, damp soil.

Much, much later, Kurt and Deke waved off the last of their friends—Frog was spending the Thanksgiving holiday with the Hightowers, Alex, Angel, Sandy and the baby, on Hilton Head. Arm in arm, they turned to go inside their new-old home. They both agreed that it was still ugly as sin, but as Kurt said, it was built to last.

"And so are we, sweetheart," he added, a familiar gleam beginning to light his one gray eye.

"Do you think Frog will be all right with the Hightowers? What if he feels out of place and decides to run off again?"

"Alex can handle him. Besides, I think he's ready to take on some polish. He knows things aren't the way they used to be."

"I hope he knows they're going to get even better," Deke mused as she followed him inside and closed the door on a perfectly splendid sunset.

"You're the expert on happy endings," Kurt whispered, taking her in his arms. "All you have to do is lead the way. I'm right behind you, sweetheart."

* * * * *

SILHOUETTE®

Desire

MAN of the MONTH 1996

He's tough enough to capture your heart,
Tender enough to cradle a newborn baby
And sexy enough to satisfy your wildest fantasies....

He's Silhouette Desire's MAN OF THE MONTH!

From the moment he meets the woman of his
dreams to the time the handsome hunk says *I do*...

Fall in love with these incredible men:

In July:	*THE COWBOY AND THE KID* by Anne McAllister
In August:	*DON'T FENCE ME IN* by Kathleen Korbel
In September:	*TALLCHIEF'S BRIDE* by Cait London
In October:	*THE TEXAS BLUE NORTHER* by Lass Small
In November:	*STRYKER'S WIFE* by Dixie Browning
In December:	*CHRISTMAS PAST* by Joan Hohl

MAN OF THE MONTH...ONLY FROM
SILHOUETTE DESIRE

MOM96JD

Take 4 bestselling love stories FREE

Plus get a FREE surprise gift!

Special Limited-time Offer

Mail to Silhouette Reader Service™

P.O. Box 609
Fort Erie, Ontario
L2A 5X3

YES! Please send me 4 free Silhouette Desire® novels and my free surprise gift. Then send me 6 brand-new novels every month, which I will receive months before they appear in bookstores. Bill me at the low price of $3.24 each plus 25¢ delivery and GST*. That's the complete price and a savings of over 10% off the cover prices—quite a bargain! I understand that accepting the books and gift places me under no obligation ever to buy any books. I can always return a shipment and cancel at any time. Even if I never buy another book from Silhouette, the 4 free books and the surprise gift are mine to keep forever.

326 BPA A3UY

Name	(PLEASE PRINT)	
Address	Apt. No.	
City	Province	Postal Code

This offer is limited to one order per household and not valid to present Silhouette Desire® subscribers. *Terms and prices are subject to change without notice. Canadian residents will be charged applicable provincial taxes and GST.

CDES-696 ©1990 Harlequin Enterprises Limited

FORTUNE'S Children™

Bestselling Author
LINDA TURNER

Continues the twelve-book series—FORTUNE'S CHILDREN—
in **November 1996** with Book Five

THE WOLF AND THE DOVE

Adventurous pilot Rachel Fortune and traditional Native American
doctor Luke Greywolf set sparks off each other the minute they met.
But widower Luke was tormented by guilt and vowed never to love
again. Could tempting Rachel heal Luke's wounded heart so they
could share a future of happily ever after?

MEET THE FORTUNES—a family whose legacy is greater than riches.
Because where there's a will…there's a *wedding!*

*A CASTING CALL TO
ALL FORTUNE'S CHILDREN FANS!*
If you are truly fortunate,
you may win a trip to
Los Angeles to audition for
Wheel of Fortune®. Look for
details in all retail Fortune's Children titles!

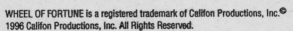

WHEEL OF FORTUNE is a registered trademark of Califon Productions, Inc.©
1996 Califon Productions, Inc. All Rights Reserved.

Look us up on-line at: http://www.romance.net   FC-5-C

For the Janos siblings

Three Weddings and a Gift

leads to a lot of loving!
Join award-winning author

Cathie Linz

as she shows how an *unusual* inheritance leads to
love at first sight—and beyond!—in

MICHAEL'S BABY #1023
September 1996

SEDUCING HUNTER #1029
October 1996

and

ABBIE AND THE COWBOY #1036
November 1996

Only from

SILHOUETTE® *Desire*®

Look us up on-line at: http://www.romance.net   3GIFT

As seen on TV!
Free Gift Offer

With a Free Gift proof-of-purchase from any Silhouette® book,
you can receive a beautiful cubic zirconia pendant.

This gorgeous marquise-shaped stone is a genuine cubic
zirconia—accented by an 18" gold tone necklace.

(Approximate retail value $19.95)

Send for yours today...
compliments of *Silhouette*®

To receive your free gift, a cubic zirconia pendant, send us one original proof-of-
purchase, photocopies not accepted, from the back of any Silhouette Romance™,
Silhouette Desire®, Silhouette Special Edition®, Silhouette Intimate Moments®
or Silhouette Yours Truly™ title available in August, September, October, November and
December at your favorite retail outlet, together with the Free Gift Certificate, plus a
check or money order for $1.65 U.S./$2.15 CAN. (do not send cash) to cover postage and
handling, payable to Silhouette Free Gift Offer. We will send you the specified gift. Allow
6 to 8 weeks for delivery. Offer good until December 31, 1996 or while quantities last.
Offer valid in the U.S. and Canada only.

Free Gift Certificate

Name: _____

Address: _____

City: _____ State/Province: _____ Zip/Postal Code: _____

Mail this certificate, one proof-of-purchase and a check or money order for postage
and handling to: SILHOUETTE FREE GIFT OFFER 1996. In the U.S.: 3010 Walden
Avenue, P.O. Box 9077, Buffalo NY 14269-9077. In Canada: P.O. Box 613, Fort Erie,
Ontario L2Z 5X3.

FREE GIFT OFFER
ONE PROOF-OF-PURCHASE

084-KMD

To collect your fabulous FREE GIFT, a cubic zirconia pendant, you must include this
original proof-of-purchase for each gift with the properly completed Free Gift Certificate.

084-KMD-R

A Funny Thing Happened on the Way to the Baby Shower...

When four college friends reunite to celebrate the arrival of one bouncing baby, they find four would-be grooms on the way!

Don't miss a single, sexy tale in

RAYE MORGAN'S

Only in

BABY DREAMS
in May '96 (SD #997)

A GIFT FOR BABY
in July '96 (SD #1010)

BABIES BY THE BUSLOAD
in September '96 (SD #1022)

And look for

INSTANT DAD, WILL TRAIN
in November '96

Only from

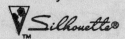

RMBS

You're About to Become a

Privileged Woman

Reap the rewards of fabulous free gifts and
benefits with proofs-of-purchase from
Silhouette and Harlequin books

Pages & Privileges™

It's our way of thanking you for
buying our books at your
favorite retail stores.

Pages & Privileges™

PROOF OF PURCHASE

SD-PP19

Offer expires March 31, 1997

Harlequin and Silhouette—
the most privileged readers in the world!

For more information about Harlequin and
Silhouette's PAGES & PRIVILEGES program call the
Pages & Privileges Benefits Desk: 1-503-794-2499

Silhouette®

SD-PP19